Who had planned the rendezvous?

Françoise checked her watch. It was five past eleven. She strained in the dim cathedral light to see who was kneeling in the seventh pew, just as the letter had instructed.

She stood motionless... as if waiting for something to happen. Ten minutes crept by: eleven-fifteen, eleven-twenty. The kneeling figure did not move.

Finally Françoise took a deep breath and silently approached him. She noticed his tall form, the strong face and clear gray eyes. He seemed familiar somehow. When their eyes finally met, Françoise was astonished to recognize Pierre. Since her father's death, she had despaired of ever seeing Pierre Lalonde again.

He handed her a letter identical to her own. "Obviously we have a mutual friend," he murmured.

The Sea Gull's letters continued to appear... luring them into a web of frightening complexity.

The Sea Gull

by JEAN D'ASTOR

Harlequin Books

NEW YORK • TORONTO

THE SEA GULL/first published November 1977

Second printing November 1977
Third printing March 1978

ISBN 0-373-90016-3

Chapter 1

Odile stood motionless, her mouth open, staring at the mantel. As she looked at the envelope resting on top of the clock, she knew that three minutes earlier no letter had been there!

She was positive. Hadn't she just finished dusting the mantel before going into the kitchen? She had left the room only long enough to check the roast that Mlle Elise had put into the oven before going out to shop. Now there was a letter where nothing had been before.

How could that possibly be? She was alone in the house and the doors were locked. No one could have come in without Odile knowing about it!

The mail had been delivered much earlier, and as usual, there had been no parcel or registered letter. The mailman had simply dropped several letters through the mail slot in the door.

In any case the envelope on the mantel had not been carried by the postal service for it bore no stamp and no street address: just the name, "Mlle Elise Topard" and the word "Personal" underlined twice.

Frowning and worried, Odile glanced around the room. Having spent forty-two years as a cleaning woman, she was not accustomed to dealing with things that required any amount of thought. She preferred two hours of physical work to ten minutes of mental activity. But under the circumstances, she felt she should make an attempt to solve the mystery.

It was obvious that unless the letter had simply flown in like a bird through the window, someone had come and gone during the short time she had been out of the room. Both possibilities seemed highly unlikely, unless . . . .

She stepped over to the window, which overlooked the garden, opened it wide and leaned out. It would have been easy for someone to enter through the window; the intruder had only to cross the ten-foot-wide flower bed that bordered the house.

But the gardener had prepared the ground for his spring planting only the day before, and there were no traces of footsteps on the well-raked soil.

Glancing around, Odile saw nothing out of place. All seemed normal, except for a sea gull resting on one of the porch pillars. Was she imagining things, or was that bird staring at her? Any other day, she wouldn't have paid any attention to the gull, but the letter had made her uneasy. Now, even quite ordinary details were troubling her.

She thought about the door to the laundry room; perhaps it had been left open. And then, there was the side entrance . . . .

She crossed the room and entered the small adjoining sitting room, where the shutters had been kept closed since the death of the lady of the house. Then she traversed the small hallway that led to the other rooms. Nothing. Everything was as usual; the doors to the outside were locked. She returned to the living room.

The sea gull had not moved from its perch. Set against the gray sky, it looked as if it had been chiseled out of granite. But as she continued to watch the bird, its eyes blinked as if it was trying to communicate with Odile. A strange feeling came over the woman. Although inclined to laugh at superstition, she could not deny her Brittany upbringing. She believed in omens.

A letter that seemed to have come out of nowhere didn't help matters. She leaned over to look at it more closely but did not touch it. A white envelope on which the name had been typed: nothing else.

Odile sighed, knowing very well that she was wasting her time. Why should she worry? After all, the letter wasn't addressed to her. She would know soon enough, when Mlle Elise opened it, if there was any cause for concern.

She resumed her work but found herself nervous and distracted. Then the vacuum cleaner started to act up. True, she had a very peculiar way of handling the machine, yanking on the cord to unplug it as if it was a leash on a stubborn dog. Nine times out of ten, the machine would follow her from room to room; but the tenth time, the cord would break.

The cord broke that morning. Now Odile became upset again, as she looked down at the dead machine—another evil omen!

And outside, the sea gull fluttered its wings as if it were applauding.

As soon as Mlle Elise came in, Odile told her about the letter.

"A letter for me? Who brought it? Did you think to check the roast?"

Among her other traits, Mlle Elise had the bad habit

of asking several questions at once. Odile had become quite used to this by now and usually solved the problem by answering only the last one.

"I lowered the heat and added some water. That's precisely when—"

"I see you've broken the cord again! I've told you at least a hundred times that you only waste time when you try to go too fast! Well, where's the letter?"

"It's on the mantel in the living room."

"What are you waiting for? Go and get it for me!"

"I think you should come with me."

Elise stopped in the midst of hanging up her coat and looked at Odile with disbelief.

"What's the matter? You sound frightened."

"No, but I don't know how it got there."

Elise had always possessed good self-control; her face rarely betrayed any emotion. She did not seem in the least affected by what the cleaning lady was saying and went on calmly arranging her coat on the hanger and putting it in the closet. She then walked to the living room and examined the letter for a minute, without touching it, just as Odile had done earlier.

"What time was it when you started cleaning this room?" she finally asked.

"As soon as you left. It must have been around ten."

"Are you sure there was nothing on the mantel when you started?"

Odile shrugged, "I moved the clock as usual to clean beneath it, and I'm neither blind nor crazy! If the letter had been there, I'd have seen it!"

"Was that window open?"

"Yes."

"Then that's how the letter was brought in."

"No."

"What do you mean, 'no'? How can you be so sure?"

"I know I'm right!" Then she added dryly, "You don't have to be a genius to figure it out!"

Odile was given the rare pleasure of seeing some confusion on her employer's face, as the latter moved to the window and looked out. One quick look at the flower bed told her that the cleaning woman was right.

"Someone must have come in by the side door, or maybe the door to the laundry room."

"I checked. They were locked."

"What about the other windows?"

"All locked."

At last, Elise seemed troubled.

"Now Odile, think! The letter can't have walked in here on its own!"

"Think about what?"

"Something must have happened while you were in the kitchen. Didn't you see or hear anything?"

"I've told you several times already! If I were you, I'd quit asking so many questions and read the letter."

Elise picked the envelope up as if it were something repulsive.

"Are you asking me to believe a bird is the only one who could have delivered this?"

As she spoke, she looked at Odile out of the corner of her eye, but the woman's face expressed only normal curiosity.

"I've considered it," replied the cleaning woman. "It may have been that sea gull perched on the pillar outside. It hasn't moved for the past hour . . . as though it's waiting for a reply. . . . "

Elise cast a slightly disgusted look at her and tore open the envelope. She pulled out a regular white sheet. At first glance, she frowned, then started to blush.

Forgetting her manners, Odile came closer, craning her neck. Elise did not react right away. She seemed hypnotized by the few typewritten lines dancing before her eyes. Her hand had started to shake.

She came to her senses when she felt the other woman's shoulder brush against hers.

"Odile! Mind your own—"

She stepped away abruptly, appearing to have regained her composure. Indicating the door with her chin, she told the woman to go and peel the potatoes for lunch.

Then in a lower tone, she told Odile never to mention the letter to anyone, saying it was just a ridiculous joke and she would be the laughing stock of the neighborhood, should she say a word. . . .

Like a robot, Odile headed toward the kitchen. Her earlier dismay at discovering the letter was nothing compared to her present state of mind. She was almost terrified.

Before sitting down to peel the potatoes, she walked to the window, looked in the direction of the porch and made the sign of the cross.

She had not been able to read the letter or even make out any of the words, but she had caught a glimpse of the bottom of the page, where a small drawing had been used as a signature. . . .

The drawing had been the outline of a sea gull.

Chapter 2

"Hello, Pierre? It's Aunt Elise. Listen, I . . . I'm sorry to bother you, but . . . could you come and have lunch with us?"

"Why? Is anything wrong?"

"Nothing serious. I'll explain when you get here."

"Has something happened to the children?"

"No, don't worry. They've just returned from school. I told them they could play in the yard until you got here."

"Are you having problems with Odile?"

"Of course not. And not with the gardener either. I simply want to ask your advice about something."

"Couldn't it wait until tonight? I promised Mireille I'd take her out for lunch. It's a little late to call her and cancel!"

"All right, let's forget it. Tonight, then. The children will be disappointed, though; they were looking forward to having lunch with you."

"I'll hardly have time to see them. They have to go back to school—"

But Elise had already hung up. That was so like her. Either she would have her way or she would forget the whole matter.

Pierre began to have second thoughts. Elise would not have called him at the office without good reason. Since she moved into his house, three years ago, she had called just once; when Michel had an appendicitis attack. Knowing that her nephew was a busy man, she would call only in an emergency.

He could cancel lunch with Mireille and instead take her out to dinner that night. She had no specific timetable to keep and would probably prefer going out to eat in the evening. The only way to find out was to call her. He dialed her number and recognized her voice right away.

"Pierre, don't tell me you have to cancel!"

"I'm afraid so, my dear Mireille. I'm terribly sorry, but. . . ."

He didn't feel that his aunt's call sounded important enough to justify canceling, so he decided to come up with something else.

" . . . there's an important client who's come in without notice. I have no choice but to take him to lunch. I apologize, but you know how business is. . . . "

"And I've been running around for the past hour trying to choose the right dress to wear!"

"Wear it tonight for dinner. Candlelight will make your dress look even nicer and I'll have more time to admire you." He added jokingly, "Maybe we can even elope!"

"Tonight?"

"Did you have something else planned for this evening?"

"No, Pierre, but . . . . "

"I see. You're afraid that you might not be allowed to go out in the evening. Would you like me to call your father and ask if it's all right?"

"You seem to forget that I'm of age! My parents treat me like an adult. And you know how much they like you. . . . Oh, that reminds me. Father asked me to tell you something, but I've forgotten what it was. Let me see now, something about containers for a dry shampoo."

"Yes, I know. It's for a new product and I've supplied him with a few samples to try out."

"Well, it's a great success. Every one of them was sold in no time. You can expect a very large order!"

"Wonderful! Then we have something to celebrate tonight! I'll pick you up at seven. It'll be much more enjoyable. This client might even prove to be a blessing. I can't really relax during the lunch hour anyway. I'm always thinking of what I've done in the morning and what I still have to do in the afternoon. In the evening, I'm much better company."

As he hung up, Pierre didn't feel too happy with himself. He was vaguely disturbed at something that seemed to be happening quite often lately in his relationship with Mireille. He couldn't quite pin down the reason, but he seemed compelled to lie to her and say things that never really expressed his true feelings.

He picked up the phone again and called home. At the other end of the line, Elise smiled triumphantly.

"You were able to get out of it? Good. Then I'll see you in half an hour? We'll be ready to eat as soon as you get here."

It was noon and the factory workers were leaving the plant. Pierre went to his window to watch his employees trickle out.

Once again, he thought about turning one of the larger rooms into a cafeteria, but most of the employees preferred to go home for lunch, even those who lived some distance away in the country. These people weren't prepared to spend an uninterrupted day at the factory.

And perhaps the number of employees didn't justify such a move; not just then, anyway. How many did he have? Sixty? Sixty-five? Thinking about his employees, Pierre sometimes felt like some sort of miserly collector. The increasing number of workers was better proof of his success than the construction site of his new plant across the road. And he had good reason to be proud, because he was providing jobs for a lot of people who might otherwise be out of work.

Another feeling, more delicate, caused him to think of his father, It was gratitude, but more precisely, satisfaction at having done something tangible with his gratitude. Unlike so many men who find it natural to sit in the boss's chair without having to work for it, Pierre was very grateful that he had never had to worry about a job; he was proud to be able to continue where his father had left off.

All this had started seventy-five years earlier, in the heart of the town. His grandfather, Antoine Lalonde, had set up a pottery shop in an old warehouse. He had worked all his life; initially by himself, then with his son, Hervé.

Later, the shop had become a store that had increased in size many times throughout the years. . . .

Hervé, Pierre's father, had opened a small factory on the outskirts of town, on the same spot where the Lalonde Corporation's very modern factory now stood. In the beginning, it had been a family enterprise, providing work for about fifteen employees.

Then it was Pierre's turn to take over the reins of the business. He had maintained the processes established long ago and remained faithful to the pottery traditions of Brittany. He had also decided to expand his line of products by making plastic items.

Well taught by his father, he was astute enough to start off in a small way and plan carefully for the future. He bought all the land adjoining the original lot and tailored his investments to the short-term needs of his production. Thus, he had required only demand loans from the banks.

And now, still in his thirties, he could boast of being the sole director and owner of a very important factory.

The yard below was now quiet again. He returned to his desk, straightened out some papers, then opened the door to the next room where his secretary sat typing.

"Aren't you going for lunch?"

"I'm just finishing this letter to the Cherrier Company. I'll be out of here in two minutes. If you want to sign it, I'll drop it off there on my way home."

Mme Rogues had been with Pierre since he'd started. In many respects, she knew the business better than he did. In her mid-forties, heavyset, quick and precise, she gave the impression of being dynamic and full of energy. She had the qualities of a good secretary—always on time, discreet, efficient, excellent memory—and also two distinct advantages: no children, and a ship's captain for a husband. He was away from home nine months of the year. . . .

Pierre often told her that it was because of her he could be free of worries whenever he had to be away from the factory. She could run the office almost as well as he could. In the event of an emergency, she would put everything on hold and try to reach him, no matter what time of day or night. And since the death of his wife, she had become his confidante and a very good friend.

As soon as he'd signed the letter, he told her about his aunt's call and that he was having lunch with her.

"I hope there's nothing wrong with the children."

"No, she wants to ask me for some advice about something or other; she wasn't too specific. I have to admit I'm puzzled."

"I can well understand that, knowing her! She never needs anyone to help her solve her problems. This one must be very difficult."

"I'll tell you about it this afternoon. By the way, what time is my appointment with the representative from the Sodelac Company?"

"Three-thirty. But remember, you also promised to see Monsieur Bellec right after lunch."

"That's right! Ask him to come about three. I should have Aunt Elise's problem solved by then."

"It can't be that serious . . . as long as it has nothing to do with the children. . . . "

Driving along the Odet River, Pierre thought about Mme Rogues' last words. She knew him well, all right. It was true: all his thoughts revolved around his children and his factory. Nothing else mattered, not even Mireille. . . .

Mireille was a touchy subject and Pierre usually tried to avoid thinking about it. He did find her extremely attractive, and it was flattering to think that a twenty-three-year-old woman had made up her mind to have him for her own, but that was not what was important.

There was another element to complicate matters. Mireille was the daughter of the man who owned the Farges Laboratories, an outfit that represented about one-third of his business!

Pierre wondered if his feelings for her went any deeper than physical attraction and his interest in keeping her father's business. He often tried to convince himself, but deep down he didn't believe there was more. In fact, he doubted his ability to feel anything more. Not for her, not for anyone.

He believed he would never be able to love again, that something in him had died forever. Had died the day Regine . . . .

He was assailed by a sudden choking sensation. Even after five years, that dreadful day could still hurt him as nothing else ever could.

Regine, with her bright smiling eyes that conveyed such warmth, such love . . . Regine was happiness personified . . . the love of his life. . . .

They had been married for six years and had had two children, three years apart: Veronique and Michel. His company had been expanding rapidly. Now, like a hungry man remembering the many times he had rejected food, he looked back on those days, regretting that he had not lived them to their fullest. Pierre always felt he should have had some premonition of disaster, instead of just uninterrupted bliss right up until the last moment . . . .

. . . the moment he had picked up the phone in his office and some strange voice, far away, had said something he couldn't really make out. The voice had asked if he was M. Lalonde . . . said something about Mme Lalonde being involved in a car accident. . . .

Regine had left that morning to visit her parents farther down the coast and was returning that night. That was all Pierre knew or wanted to know. But the voice had continued, and still Pierre couldn't make out what was being said, didn't want to understand. He asked the person to repeat every word; then he repeated the words himself, like someone who had lost his senses. The words were simple, yet so horrible.

" . . . In the hospital . . . serious . . . hasn't regained consciousness . . . must go right away. . . ."

Pierre could now recall every detail of those hours

that had marked the collapse of his life. It had been October, nightfall, the wind whipping the ocean and ripping apart the clouds. . . .

There had been no one in the factory, except the night watchman who was just coming on duty. Pierre had felt very much alone. He had known that it was all over.

"She hasn't regained consciousness. . . . "

When he had called Odile to tell her to give the children dinner and put them to bed without waiting for their mother, his voice had not broken. While driving to the hospital, he had summoned the strength to compose himself.

"It's raining, the road is slippery; I have to drive carefully; I must not take risks. . . . "

He was to learn later than Regine had died by the time he received the phone call.

Even today, he was still surprised that the brutal shock had not changed him. Athletic, tall and slim, with clear gray eyes and brown hair that had only a suggestion of gray at the temples, he was still young-looking.

Only he knew how old he felt, despite outward appearances. Old age is something that happens to everybody else, and one does not count the passing years. But growing old is counting the number of people who die around us. And for Pierre, there was first his father, then his wife, and later his mother. . . .

Today, nothing had really changed, nothing visible. He was still running his business with the same enthusiasm, the same friendliness toward his employees. Everyone thought that the years had succeeded in easing his sorrow. They even wondered why a man of his age, so successful in business, had never remarried.

"He lives with his mother's sister," people would

say, "an old, miserable spinster! That's no way for such a man to live!"

Strangely enough, Pierre often told himself the same thing, but in a detached manner, as though he were talking about someone else! Generating interest in his own future required a great deal of effort.

Remarry? Why not? Living alone could be rather difficult for a young industrialist, especially in a small town with its numerous social obligations.

Mireille might be the logical answer. Though somewhat superficial, she liked to entertain and would be a perfect hostess. And because of her age, the children would perhaps consider her an older sister.

However, the relationship between Mireille and Aunt Elise might present some difficulties. Then again, maybe not. Mireille showed no interest in cooking and keeping house; she would be only too happy to let the older woman run the household.

Pierre had only one real objection: the lack of love between them. Could he really marry someone, not out of love but because his home needed a mistress? It was too much like hiring a secretary.

Such a liaison would be dishonest. Their life together would be a permanent lie.

WHEN HE ARRIVED at the house, lunch was served.

"I'm warning you, Veronique, you will not leave the table until you've eaten all your potatoes!"

"I'm not hungry any more, Aunt Elise!"

"Really? Too bad! I was planning to serve chocolate mousse for dessert."

Veronique looked imploringly at her father now seated at the table, but Pierre turned away.

"If I were to let her have her way," Elise said to him, "she would eat nothing but candy and junk food. Michel, your elbows! A well-mannered person doesn't eat with his elbows on the table!"

"Daddy has his elbows on the table!"

Pierre quickly changed position.

"Your father is not a little boy; he can do what he wants. And watch your tongue or I'll send you to bed!"

Michel knew she meant it. Better not argue until after the chocolate mousse. As his aunt turned to get the dessert, Michel shrugged and looked toward his father for support. Pierre just frowned; right now, it wouldn't take much to start Aunt Elise on the warpath.

Pierre sighed. Once more, he would return to his office edgy and nervous. His many trips and business meetings permitted him few opportunities to have meals with his children. And the time he could spare was not enough to allow him to get to know them better and win their confidence.

Also, Aunt Elise's philosophy of quick justice always cast stormy weather over the group. Scoldings, warnings, threats of punishment. . . . Michel had not washed his hands; Veronique was dropping food on her dress. An overturned glass was a major catastrophe. Something was always wrong.

Pierre felt bad about the situation. Elise would never see things his way, and the children always felt he was on her side. In keeping his neutrality, he felt as if he was betraying everyone.

"Funny, isn't it, how they seem to misbehave on purpose whenever you're around," she would say.

Today's lunch was not as bad as some. Elise, who seemed preoccupied, was not as picky as usual. Pierre was still wondering what she wanted to talk to him about.

"We'll discuss it after lunch," she said.

Pierre assumed she wanted his advice on some investment or other. No matter what his advice might be, however, she would go ahead with what she had decided on in the first place. She had quite a bit of money of her own and never knew what to do with it. And since moving in with Pierre, she hardly spent a sou.

"Cheese, anyone?"

As she returned to the kitchen, Pierre watched her with a smile on his face. Small frame, very delicate, always busy, she inevitably wore a black dress, cinched tightly at the waist. She reminded him of an ant, a giant ant. He could picture her very well carrying a load twice or three times her size.

And, like an ant, she never stopped. She always served the meals, constantly running back and forth from kitchen to dining room, telling Odile and the children what to do all at the same time. She could do the work of several servants. She had tried several maids, none of whom lasted more than a week. Those with backbone handed in their aprons; the others were thrown out. . . .

After thirty-two years, Odile was quite secure in the house, but then, she was something of an institution and could not be shaken by Elise's dictatorship.

Adrian, the gardener and handyman, had the advantage of belonging to what Elise considered the dominant sex. She had a little respect and admiration for him, particularly since the day he'd threatened to throw her out of a second-floor window if she didn't stop aggravating him. . . .

Pierre's feelings for his aunt were a mixture of esteem, gratitude and affection, all seasoned with irritation. Certainly she rendered him a great service by looking after the house and his children. But in the latter respect, Elise was not the best solution.

She had never had children of her own. More than anything else, she viewed his son and daughter as little animals that had to be trained according to certain undisputed principles. Although she loved them in her own way, she was unable to show them any affection. The continued strife between Elise and her charges must surely do irreparable damage to the not fully formed personalities of the children.

They needed someone young to look after them, someone who could guide them, yet whose authority would be exercised with tenderness. Pierre tried to imagine Mireille in the role. Would she be equal to the task of helping the children grow up properly?

Veronique had finally managed to eat all her potatoes.

"We had movies at school today, papa."

"You have all the luck! When I was your age, we had to work every morning."

"It wasn't an ordinary movie with words; we saw flowers opening like magic."

Pierre noticed the way his children seemed to relax as soon as Aunt Elise was out of the room.

Even with her light hair, Veronique looked very much like her father. She had the same gray eyes and regular features, the same pensive expression. She was only ten, yet she was somehow motherly in her attitude toward her younger brother.

Michel was a sports enthusiast; hair always a mess, good physique, well-tanned—a soccer player in the making.

"I did some painting today," he announced.

"Did you? Pretty soon, I'll be able to hire you in the factory. Are you good at it?"

"Not really! I was doing all right at first, but then I pressed too hard and the egg broke."

"The egg? You mean you're painting eggs at school?"

Veronique interrupted to explain.

"It's for Easter. When I was little, the teacher used to have us decorate eggs."

Michel agreed. "That's right. And she also told us not to say anything at home, because it's supposed to be a surprise!"

"What a dummy! Why are you talking about it, if it's a surprise?" Veronique was quite offended at the little boy's indiscretion.

Michel pouted. All this fuss about a stupid egg that didn't interest him in the slightest. Anyway, Aunt Elise was coming back with the chocolate mousse. No one spoke for the rest of the meal.

When the children had gone, Pierre asked his aunt why she wanted to see him so urgently.

"Before we get to that, I must tell you that this house is haunted!" She sounded very sure of herself.

"Fascinating! You met a ghost?"

"No, not yet, but I'm sure there is one. Unless you believe in the legend of the sea gulls."

"What legend?"

"How can you, a native of Brittany, ask that? Don't you know about the sea gulls that carry messages from men on the high seas to their waiting wives and sweethearts?"

Leaving Veronique in the living room, where she had to practice piano, Elise and Pierre entered the small adjacent sitting room. Through the smoke from his cigarette, Pierre was worriedly observing his aunt.

"Ghosts, sea gulls. . . . I must confess I don't have a clue about what you're getting at!"

"I'm talking about the anonymous letter I received this morning."

"From the postman?"

"That's precisely *not* the way I got it! Look at the envelope. I don't have any idea at all how it got here! Unless . . . . Anyway, read it first. I'll tell you afterward what I think."

Pierre's eyes were drawn to the little sketch at the bottom of the page.

"Now I see why you were talking about sea gulls. At least, you're lucky in one way! Sea gulls aren't nearly as scary as ravens. Now, let's see what danger or what treason the messenger is trying to warn you about."

He read slowly.

There are things not done that are worse than actions; silences worse than slander.

You were the secretary of Maurice Lachenaire. The night of his death, you witnessed certain things, noticed certain disappearances for which you suspected the reason. But you had no proof. It was therefore wise of you not to mention anything.

Today it would be cowardice. Events have confirmed your suspicions. You no longer have the right to remain silent. The happiness of many people is in jeopardy.

Immediately below the tiny picture, the note was signed "The Sea Gull."

Chapter 3

Pierre handed the letter back to his aunt.

"A classic example. Sententious generalities, allusions to facts about things that happened many years ago and now are impossible to verify. I suppose there's not a word of truth in this letter?"

"Not one that is false, I'm afraid. Every sentence expresses my own feelings and thoughts exactly!"

"What? You mean—"

"I'll explain everything in a minute. First, I want to tell you how I think this letter got in here. If I'm to believe Odile, it was brought by a ghost or a sea gull! Funny coincidence, but there was a sea gull on the porch at just the right time!"

Elise repeated word for word everything Odile had told her. Pierre asked the same questions she had asked. Being a pragmatic person, he reached his own conclusions.

"One way or another, someone very real came in.

There must be a simple explanation; we just haven't figured it out yet."

"There's only one that I can come up with: Odile lied. I think she invented the whole thing!" Elise spoke with conviction.

"Odile? Invent something like that?"

"Well, maybe not. She could never concoct such a tale on her own. Whoever gave her the letter probably told her what to say."

"But to what end? Why would anyone make it so complicated? It's the fastest way to raise suspicion. Besides, do you really think anyone in his right mind would take Odile into his confidence? That woman is so simpleminded, she'd be talking about it right away!"

"What other explanation could there be?" Elise was truly bewildered.

"I'll repeat myself. Someone must have entered the house. Either a door wasn't locked properly or whoever it was had a duplicate key. I'll admit that these possibilities seem unlikely. Why would somebody take such risks when it would have been so simple just to mail the letter? Mind you, people who write anonymous letters usually aren't operating rationally."

"Just the same, I think the letter writer means well. Don't you agree?"

"That remains to be seen." Pierre was trying to be logical. "An anonymous letter is always a little suspicious, even when it's intended to right a wrong. This 'sea gull' seems to be less interested in somebody's happiness, as he says, than he is in making life miserable for others!"

"That's possible, yes. . . . I hadn't thought about it that way. But, even if you're right, justice should still be done."

"Tell me about it. I liked the Lachenaire family very much and I was upset about what happened: the sudden death, the confusion of the estate that wound up being bankrupt. Poor Maurice! He was a researcher, not a businessman."

Elise was annoyed. "I should've expected that from you! That's the kind of reasoning that always makes me angry!"

"You're not going to tell me that—"

"Listen, my dear nephew! I worked for seventeen years with Maurice Lachenaire. I was to him what Madame Rogues is to you. I knew him very well. He was not really a businessman because he didn't always know the 'rules of the game': accounting and financing didn't interested him. He always believed, and rightly so, that those things were better handled by the experts. He was there to conduct his experiments in the laboratory. That's why he left all the financial arrangements to Farges, who was better qualified to perform the administrative duties. But, on the other hand, Lachenaire had an acute sixth sense. He knew instinctively what the public wanted and could forecast changes in taste. I never knew him to be wrong. And you know as well as I do that in cosmetics, forecasting is a very tricky business."

"But his products never were big items on the market. Since Farges took over the business, things seem to have skyrocketed."

"Well, there you are! There's the story in a nutshell. . . . at least, that's how it looks. Everyone else sees it that way, too. Now let me straighten out a few things. Twenty years ago Maurice Lachenaire did exactly what you're doing now. When he took over the business from his father, he knew he had to develop new products if he wanted to be successful. So, for two decades he experimented with new products for the future. . . ."

"Too bad he neglected the commercial side of his business."

"But he didn't neglect it! He was doing well enough to stay in business for twenty years; quietly, but with a fair profit. No one ever doubted his capabilities!"

"That's true! I couldn't believe he was almost bankrupt when he died."

"How do you think I felt? I had no idea he was having difficulties. On the contrary, Lachenaire was extremely optimistic. He used to tell me—in the utmost secrecy—about all the new products he had finally perfected. Then all of a sudden he was dead. And when the financial statements were audited, they showed the business to be in a very sad state. Apparently he had invested greatly in an expansion program and the banks would have had to intervene for the business to continue. But banks always want guarantees or, at the very least, proof of projected income. That was the final blow: there were no new products in production!"

"What? But you were just saying —"

"I'm telling you, there weren't any! No new products, no new formulas, no papers with the smallest mention of any new product!"

"Come now, none of this is making much sense. Lachenaire was a brilliant chemist, not a madman. He wouldn't have told you—"

"The morning of his death, his safe was sealed. When it was opened in front of legal representatives, it contained only papers of little interest and certainly nothing of value."

"But Farges must have been aware of his research!"

"Farges knew nothing."

"Though he worked with Lachenaire for at least ten years?"

"He was suddenly unable to remember anything. Must have been the grief of losing his employer. . . . "

"What are you driving at?"

Elise hesitated before continuing. She picked up the letter Pierre had put on a side table.

"This . . . this Sea Gull," she whispered, "seems to know many things. I wonder how?"

She read the letter aloud slowly, pronouncing each word carefully.

" ' . . . You witnessed certain things, noticed certain disappearances. . . . ' How could he know? No one saw me that night, I'm sure. The only one I saw was . . . . At any rate, this is a lie, I didn't really see anything. It was only the following day that it came to me. . . . "

"Listen, Aunt Elise, I would appreciate your being more precise. Stop thinking out loud; you don't even know I'm here!"

"You're wrong. As a matter of fact, I'm thinking about you . . . and your business association with Farges . . . and your relationship with his daughter."

"What does Mireille have to do with this?"

"Nothing, I'm sure. As far as I can tell, she's not aware of anything."

"Aware of what? For God's sake, tell me what you're talking about!"

"To make things easier, I'll simply tell you what happened. You know how Lachenaire died?"

"Heart failure? I seem to remember he collapsed suddenly at his desk."

"That's right. But he didn't die then and there. Doctor Guillou, who arrived shortly after the emergency call, treated him, and Lachenaire was taken home. His heartbeat had returned to normal and everyone thought it wasn't too serious. Certainly that's what I thought. I left for home worried and furious at Lachenaire. For months I had been telling him to take it easy; the doctor had recommended a holiday, but he wouldn't take the time off—later, always later, he said. This time, I told myself I'd make him listen . . . but I had no way of knowing I would never see him alive again. At nine o'clock, he telephoned me at home. He sounded all right. He was calling to tell me that he had left some green personnel files on his desk.

"These contained confidential reports on some of our young employees who had had problems with the law before coming to work for us. We'd hired them on a trial basis, as part of a special program with the Department of Justice. Lachenaire took social responsibilities seriously; he agreed to give them a chance, to help them get back on the right path. No one, besides Farges, Monsieur Lachenaire and me, knew about those reports. They contained family and medical histories, information about the sentences the men had served and recommendations of the court. If those papers were to fall into the hands of other employees, you can imagine the kind of gossip that would have gone around the plant. Those poor boys only wanted a chance to go straight, and that information in the wrong hands could have caused them a great deal of harm."

"Not to mention the possibility of blackmail!" Pierre was now listening carefully to what his aunt was saying.

"Of course. I could well understand Lachenaire's concern. To reassure him, I said that I had put them away before leaving the office. But, in all the commotion, I had forgotten about them. In any case, he wanted me to get the documents and bring them to my home. He said he'd feel more secure knowing the files were out of there, since he'd be away from the office for a while."

"Five minutes later, I was in my car and on my way to the plant. I wasn't going to wait until morning. I wouldn't have slept all night! I felt responsible for leaving them on the desk. Fortunately, the commotion had taken place shortly before closing time. Except for the cleaning women, it wasn't likely that anyone would have entered the office. You know where the laboratory is—at nine-thirty at night, there's not a soul to be seen in that district. I drove around the building and parked the car at the side, because I had a key to the side door. Just as I was about to get out of the car, a man came out of the building, looked right and left and walked away very quickly. Then I heard a car drive off. It was Farges. He had walked past without seeing me, but I recognized him right away. I even recognized his heavy black briefcase."

"The personnel files had disappeared?"

"No, they were still on the desk. I took them and later gave them to Madame Lachenaire."

Once again, Elise glanced down at the letter in her hand.

"As you can see, the Sea Gull is exaggerating. I couldn't really be sure exactly what documents had disappeared. Nevertheless, the next morning, when I saw that the safe was empty. . . . "

"Farges knew the combination?"

"Of course. He was Lachenaire's right-hand man! Personally, I didn't like him, but I couldn't accuse him of anything. How could I prove it?"

"Would he have stolen the formulas even before he knew that Lachenaire was dead?"

"What risk was there? All he would've had to do was put them back in the safe, if Lachenaire got better. And if not, he'd be the only one who could run the business, since he was the only one with the information necessary to keep the factory going. That's exactly what happened!"

There was a moment of silence during which Veronique's piano playing could be heard from the next room. Pierre walked to the window and watched Michel riding his tricycle at full speed in the yard.

"All of this happened four years ago, but I still remember every detail. I've even begun to think like Farges—I know his every move and I can predict what he'll do next!"

"You'd better be careful what you say, Aunt Elise. You know, some of this might be only a product of your imagination."

"That's what I thought, at first. But then, everything went and is still going on in such a way that there is no longer any doubt in my mind. Everything has happened just the way I suspected it might from that very first night—the night I saw Farges sneaking out of the plant."

"What do you mean, 'Everything has happened just the way you suspected it might'?"

"After Lachenaire's death, Farges became his successor. But, there was a problem. Madame Lachenaire was the majority shareholder and she had two chidren. The boy was just beginning his pharmaceutical studies, and of course, it was expected that he would one day want to take his father's place in the lab. On the other hand, Farges also had two children. One was thirteen, and his father would naturally want to find him a position one day. Of course, the answer was for Farges to buy out the shares held by the Lachenaire family. Madame Lachenaire had to be convinced the business was going downhill and she'd be better off to sell out. I'm not sure how he did it, but knowing Farges's financial genius, it must have been child's play for him to give Madame Lachenaire the worst possible picture of the situation. Perhaps he mentioned tied-up investments but didn't bother to explain about long-term deals with suppliers. . . ."

"Madame Lachenaire should have consulted experts!"

"Yes, she should have; but she was completely shattered by the sudden death of her husband and was a desperate woman. And she had the greatest confidence in Farges. How could she ever imagine that he would take advantage of her state of mind to cheat her, to rob her blind?"

"I find it hard to believe! It seems so incredible. . . . "

"The second thing he had to do was lie low. Just to be on the safe side Farges waited for two years, and this was all the time he needed to get organized. He created a dummy company to buy up all the shares held by the Lachenaire family. Then, he became the sole proprietor. The banks had confidence in him; he was a financier, knew how to run a business. He had his own ideas on how to go about it: he announced his plan to undertake a mammoth research program to come up with new products. Now we come to the third stage, the one in effect right now. Maurice Lachenaire's work of twenty years will soon make a fortune for his successor!"

Pierre shook his head in disbelief.

"A plant that develops beauty products is not like a plant that produces atomic weapons! The secrets are not so closely guarded. Suppose Farges did take the documents from the safe. Other people in the plant must have been aware of Lachenaire's work. You told me just a little while ago that he talked about it with you!"

"Yes, but only in very general terms, the same way he probably discussed it with his wife and children. What if you were to come up with a new product, perhaps a new process for manufacturing plastics? Would you explain all the chemical and physical details to us?"

"Lachenaire had an assistant; he didn't conduct his experiments all by himself. You know the one I

mean—tall and slim, with graying hair? I can't think of
his name. Pernet? Perret?"

"Perrelet. An expert chemist. He's still working in
the lab."

"Really! Wouldn't you think he'd know about the
secret formulas? What does he think of all this?"

"I don't know."

"Wasn't he surprised when the safe was found to be
empty? Didn't he say anything?"

"I don't remember. I was pretty upset at the time."

"Didn't you ever mention any of your, uh, suspicions to him?"

"I hardly saw him after that. Now he works for
Farges."

Aunt Elise seemed to be embarrassed, and she hesitated before going on.

"He's the head of the lab."

"Well, well; now I see! This changeover was very re-
warding for him. With Farges, his situation improved."

Elise lowered her head in a gesture that seemed to
say, "Yes, but it doesn't prove anything."

Neither could ignore the new direction the affair was
taking. New suspicions were forming in their minds,
suspicions they could not yet fully express.

Pierre nervously lit another cigarette.

"What you have just told me is very serious. If that's
really how things happened —"

"I'm positive! Farges is a swindler!" Elise fairly
shouted the words, as she waved the letter in the air.
"And I'm not the only one who thinks so! Whoever
wrote this letter knows what's been going on as well as
I do, better than I do, perhaps! I've tried to think of all
the people I was working with at the time, but I just
can't see who it could be."

"You never mentioned anything to anybody?"

"Never!"

"Are you sure?"

"Listen, Pierre, you know I'm not the kind of woman who talks through her hat. In the past four years have I said one word about this to you? Even when you were boasting about all Farges's fine qualities?"

"I considered—and still consider—him to be a very good friend until he's proven otherwise."

"And an even better customer!"

"I'm not denying that. We have the best rapport on all levels, and I would be very disappointed—on all levels—if what you have been saying proves to be right."

"Do you really believe I'm wrong?"

Pierre looked away.

"I don't know. I must admit it looks a little bizarre."

He kept looking out the window as he continued to speak.

"Are you corresponding with Madame Lachenaire?"

"Very rarely these days. The last letter goes back to the holidays—almost three months ago, now."

"Is she still living in Paris with her children?"

"Yes. George is still studying; this is his third or fourth year in pharmacy and Françoise does private tutoring at home."

"How come? Surely they don't need the money. Mrs. Lachenaire must have made a tidy sum when she sold her shares."

"Not so! Farges arranged it so she received very little. From what I can understand, he must have played around with the books to make it look as though the plant was almost bankrupt."

"This is becoming more and more interesting. Now we have more than a petty swindler! Isn't there some way she could prove otherwise? Has she no legal recourse?"

"None. Everything was done quite legally. Nobody

forced her to sell. Now she knows she made a very serious mistake by trusting Farges so blindly. Mind you, she's not completely destitute. The sale of their house allowed her to buy an apartment in Paris, but the three of them have to live on a small income."

"Why did she move to Paris?"

"Pride. If you were a woman, you wouldn't ask that question. Can you imagine her staying here, after losing her social status, as well as a dear husband? Too many unhappy memories. Not to mention that she would be continually running into Farges!"

Staring into space, his features marred by a frown, Pierre remained for a long while leaning against the window frame. He didn't even notice Michel waving at him each time he passed in front of the window. The tinkling of the piano keys could still be heard from the living room.

When she finally broke the silence Elise seemed almost timid.

"What do you think I should do?"

"Nothing. Nothing at all! You must be very careful. This anonymous letter is worrying me more and more all the time. It could be a trap set by someone who wants to create a scandal."

Pierre looked at his watch.

"We'll talk about it later. I must get back to the office. Try to forget about this in the meantime; this Lachenaire thing really isn't any of your business, and you shouldn't be troubling yourself about it."

"But still, I was with Monsieur Lachenaire for almost twenty years; his wife thinks of me as her friend. . . . "

"So what? You're not in any position to see that justice is carried out."

"The letter only mentions evidence."

"And you are to give evidence of what and to whom? Think about it for a second. Can you see yourself telling people that Farges is a crook, that he did this and that four years ago? You'd wind up in court charged with slander. Besides, the Sea Gull certainly waited long enough to bring this thing into the open. If he knows so much, why doesn't he do something himself? Why ask you to get mixed up in it?"

Pierre walked toward the door. Elise's eyes followed him with almost a look of regret. Apparently their conversation had done nothing to ease her mind.

'I'm wondering," she ventured, "if I should give this letter to the police."

"And get the whole town in an uproar? That's precisely what the Sea Gull wants, and I'm not sure it would have the desired effect. The commissioner will simply say that the letter doesn't really amount to anything. It contains no accusation or threat. It's been written in such a way that the writer, if he was identified, would have nothing to fear. Even if you tell your story and the commissioner agrees that Farges is a most sordid type of businessman, no charges have ever been laid, so there's nothing the police can do."

As he grasped the doorknob, he added. "I'll be very surprised if the Sea Gull stops here. Farges should get a letter pretty soon, if he hasn't received one already. I'll be seeing him tonight when I pick up Mireille for dinner."

"You don't really believe that he'd tell you anything?"

"Of course not; but I'll know if he seems more nervous or worried than usual."

"You must hate me for telling you all this, because of your relationship with him . . . with her. . . . "

"If things go as I expect they will, the whole town will know soon. But for the time being, I know nothing; I haven't even been talking to you. At any rate, I don't see why this should change anything between Mireille and me! She has nothing to do with this. Where did you put my coat?"

"I put it where it belongs."

This was a sort of ritual, a silent conflict: every time Pierre came home for lunch, he would throw his coat on a chair or sofa near the door. He would no sooner start to walk away than his aunt would hang it up at the very back of the closet.

This time, she went and got it herself. The fact that she had never done so before was proof enough that she was thoroughly upset.

"Whatever wrongs a man may have done, it's not always good to bring them out in the open. Despite the legend, this Sea Gull of yours is a messenger of bad news. I have the feeling that something disturbing is beginning."

He lowered his voice as he added, "And please, don't mention it to anyone else. I just hope that Odile won't be running around town saying you've received an anonymous letter."

"I'll make up a story that should keep her quiet."

"The children didn't notice anything?"

"They weren't back from school."

It was now quiet in the living room; Veronique must have stopped to leaf through her book, *Favorite Classics*.

Apparently she found a piece she wanted to practice, for in a moment the piano was heard again, the notes following one another in a somewhat jerky fashion. Pierre and his aunt looked at each other, mutual bewilderment reflected in their expressions.

Veronique was playing Beethoven's "Fuer Elise"— "Letter for Elise"!

Chapter 4

Whether it was an old war injury, or just a stiff neck, the maître d' didn't seem to be able to turn his head without moving his whole torso.

"Just like Eric von Stroheim," whispered Pierre. "I'd swear we're in an old spy movie."

"Like who?"

"An old Austrian actor who was very big a few years ago. Probably before your time."

There he was again, talking as though he were an old man. That was the kind of talk he should be trying to avoid! Why did he always bring up the difference in their ages? What did it matter that he was fifteen years older? By the time Mireille was thirty, everyone would agree they were a perfect match.

Tonight however, she did look like a girl on her first date, in a short dress with its provocative, rather plunging neckline. Watching her descend the stairs in her parents' home, Pierre wondered how Farges felt about his daughter going out with a thirty-seven-year-old man. Thank God, as far as his own daughter was concerned, he would not have to worry about such things for many years. . . .

This kind of thinking was not helping to make him feel any younger! Pierre must have been old-fashioned; as far as Farges was concerned, the whole affair was quite correct. He smiled wryly at himself; here he was, the seducer, concerning himself about the dress of the young woman he found so attractive.

He had decided they would dine outside Quimper, their home town, and had selected a very good restaurant in Concarneau, where they would not be likely to run into anyone they knew.

As luck would have it, they hadn't been there five minutes when Doctor Guillou walked in with his wife and another couple. As they discreetly nodded to each other, the doctor glanced appreciatively at Mireille.

Pierre was flattered. As the evening progressed, he couldn't help feeling proud of his date. She knew how to dress to impress every man in the place, and if there's one thing a man likes to see, it's the admiration of other men for the woman he's with—simple male ego.

Their table was close to the fireplace. The glow of the flames danced gently on Mireille's cheeks and shoulders and lent fascinating highlights to her black hair. In this light, she seemed even more beautiful, somehow wrapped in mystery. Pierre had never seen her look more attractive.

Mireille may have looked as pretty as a picture, but Pierre seemed unable to communicate with her. Despite all his efforts, he felt he might as well have been talking to himself.

He wondered if it was the rather pretentious atmosphere of the dining room that was responsible. Mireille seemed to chatter about nothing and kept making silly little comments. And even after half a bottle of champagne had been consumed, the situation did not improve.

More than once, Pierre started to ask her if there was anything bothering her. Had her father already received a letter? Probably not; even if he had, Mireille was not likely to know about it.

Her father had seemed to behave as usual: slightly irritated with his wife, caustic with the servants and a little too jovial with Pierre.

Pierre always felt that Farges's familiarity was somewhat forced. He had a way of talking to Pierre, his hand resting on the younger man's shoulder, forcing him to sit down in one of his large wing-backed chairs as he shoved a drink into his hand, without even asking if a drink was wanted. Tonight was no exception.

His conversation had been a little too patronizing.

"So, my dear boy, Mireille told you about the powder containers? I hope your people are ready to put in a little overtime!"

That dry powder shampoo must certainly have been one of the products Maurice Lachenaire had perfected before his death. Aunt Elise was right: relations with Farges would be rather strained from now on. Pierre tried hard not to think that he was dealing with a swindler and a cheat, but he couldn't cast the idea from his mind.

Farges's tone had remained unchanged throughout their conversation.

"What's wrong? The news doesn't seem to please you at all."

"I'm sorry, I was just thinking about my production schedule: you know, a typical supplier, worried about not being able to meet his commitments." Even Pierre could hear the false ring of his words.

But Farges was oblivious. "I've just sent you an order for two million containers. Don't worry, delivery is spread over a six-month period, unless of course, sales exceed my predictions."

Pierre had made all the appropriate noises—thanks and congratulations on the success of Farges's new product—though he wondered if he'd overdone it a bit.

"You really are a phenomenon!" he'd said to Farges. "It is rare indeed, to find such an excellent combination of financial know-how and creativity in one man."

Farges basked in the warmth of Pierre's compliment, quietly sipping his drink and nodding his head.

"I have to admit that handling money has given me a very good sixth sense. . . . "

Exactly what Elise had said about Maurice Lachenaire! Pierre decided to take advantage of the opportunity to make a comment.

"That's just where Lachenaire failed; he was more of a technician."

Farges hadn't reacted. In fact, he ignored the comment altogether. In any case, he'd shown no sign of distress; hadn't even noticed Pierre staring at him.

"You see, my boy," Farges had said in his most sincere tone, "I've always pitied chemists, engineers and all of those people who think it is their mission to make their scientific knowledge useful to mankind. Contrary to what most people believe, the realm of science, in whatever field you care to consider, is very limited. It soon becomes a merry-go-round, with the researchers at a loss as to where to turn next. You can't expect them all to be like Claude Bernard or Fleming! Therefore, someone must know how to reap financial gain from their discoveries."

Pierre wondered why Farges had delivered his little speech. In minimizing Lachenaire's work, was Farges trying to ease his own conscience by claiming the merit belonged to the one who could use the knowledge to turn a profit?

Another question came to Pierre's mind: would Farges have spoken so casually if he had received a letter from the Sea Gull?

At that point in their conversation, Mme Farges had entered the room, a simpering expression on her face.

"How nice to see you. And to think you're spending a whole evening with our little girl! I hope she won't keep you waiting too long. All these young girls are the same: they never think they look pretty enough to go out with the man they, well, let's say, admire!"

Mme Farges was younger than her husband, but she looked ten years older despite—or perhaps because of—her bleached hair, heavy makeup and tendency to overdress. Every time he saw her, Pierre couldn't help worrying a little.

As long as Mireille doesn't turn out to be like her mother, he would think to himself.

He chose to believe instead that Mireille was more like her father, a good-looking man in spite of his rounded features and thinning hair.

Mme Farges hadn't shown the least sign of concern or anxiety. She'd been her usual uninteresting self, repeating the same old stuff, and ignoring her husband's exasperated looks.

Pierre had had the impression he was seeing them for the first time as they really were. M. Farges, an upstart in the business world, having come a long way since starting as an accountant in a jelly-processing plant, and his wife, putting on airs, trying desperately to hide the fact that her parents had owned a roadside diner on the outskirts of town.

Until now, Pierre had liked them because they seemed to be simple people from honest, working-class families, not unlike himself. But now, he noticed how vulgar they really were and deep inside, he could not feel any real sympathy for them. He would never have considered becoming very friendly with them anyway, not because of the age difference, but because of some instinctive feeling that warned him to be wary. . . .

Pierre had been relieved when Mireille had finally come down. After they left the house, he wondered if her parents had noticed anything different about him.

He had tried very hard to hide any sign of his discomfort in their presence. But Aunt Elise's words had kept flashing back at him.

"Farges is a swindler. . . . "

He was trying to clear up the situation in his own mind. *Perhaps the whole thing was just the old girl's imagination*, he wondered. Maybe the letter pertained to something completely different. . . . What others did was none of his business . . . and, anyway, it was all past history. Pierre also had to face the fact that he was in a rather precarious position, as far as Farges was concerned: his own plant was doing very well because of Farges's orders; his expansion allowed Pierre to expand, too. . . .

But then, the silhouette of a man rushing through the night, clutching a black briefcase, would jump to his mind . . . along with the thought of a despondent woman closing a door behind her, having to leave what had been hers all her life. . . .

The maître d' was standing behind Mireille. He resembled nothing so much as a robot, and it was almost a surprise to hear him talk.

"Madame would like more lobster canapés?"

But Mireille was not interested in the delicacies. Trying to make himself useful, the man poured more champagne into their glasses, with great precision and a kind of reverence.

Pierre signaled him to bring another bottle.

As the maître d' left the table, Pierre looked at Mireille.

"Maybe now we'll have five minutes to ourselves."

Mireille was looking distractedly around the room, as if she hadn't heard her companion. He finally attracted her attention and asked if she had been in the restaurant before.

"No, but I've heard a lot about it. It's supposed to be one of the best."

"I'd say that whoever decorated it must have bought every antique within a radius of fifty miles!"

Copper, ceramics and brass items hung from the walls. Every table had a lamp and some flowers: definitely decor for wealthy tourists. This was not the kind of place Pierre would normally take his friends for dinner. He preferred the simpler eating places along the coast, where the food was far superior. But he knew Mireille's love of luxurious surroundings.

The important thing to a woman, he said to himself, *is that it costs money; preferably a lot!*

Then he was angry with himself for having such thoughts. After all, he had selected the restaurant. He should have been happy that Mireille was enjoying it, and that he was in the company of such a beautiful young woman. And she did look beautiful, with her classic features and long silky hair!

Pierre became aware that his youth was practically over; soon he would simply become a money-making machine. Maybe he was a little envious of Mireille's youth, because he was not able to share with her the things that belonged to youth. To be able to talk of little nothings ... innocently. ...

Pierre was trying in vain to find a topic of conversation about which they both could express their ideas and feelings. She would hum popular songs; he didn't know the name of a single popular singer. She was interested in fan magazines; he read history and travel books. She would go to the movies twice a week; the only film he had seen in the past year was a Walt Disney production, and then, he had gone only to please Veronique. . . .

"Have you seen the Valettes lately?"

"Mother and I were there for tea last week."

"Was Paula still in St. Moritz?"

"She had just come home. Not even tanned! It seems the weather was terrible the whole time she was there."

"You say that as though you're happy about it."

"Well, I'm sorry on her account, but glad for myself. I was supposed to go there for the Easter break with Antoine, but that idiot didn't get his marks at college, so papa cut off his expense money!"

"Is your brother lazy?"

"Well, I wouldn't say he's lazy. He just doesn't like to study, that's all. Papa refuses to accept that."

Well, that was news! That could jeopardize all of Farges's plans. He couldn't rely on the future success of his son to justify his own behavior, should he find it necessary one day to do so. . . .

They fell silent again. Antoine's affairs were not very interesting. His back to the rest of the dining room, Pierre could not see the other guests, but once in a while Doctor Guillou's hearty laughter could be heard above the buzz of voices. Mireille seemed to be acting rather coyly, and Pierre realized that she must be the recipient of many covert glances from the other diners. He knew she was aware of them, although she was pretending otherwise.

It wasn't the first time. Normally Pierre would have found it charming, part of her innocence. But today, he felt that Mireille was being indifferent to him.

He felt sure she was angry with him for something,

and when the silence threatened to continue for a little too long, he decided to ask.

"Something seems to be bothering you, Mireille. I have the feeling you're bored."

"No, just a little tired. I spent the whole afternoon shopping."

"Then you would rather have had lunch?"

"Speaking of lunch, you haven't told me how it went with your client at noon."

Something in her tone warned Pierre she knew more than she was saying.

"You didn't ask."

Mireille shrugged, waited a moment; then she demanded, "Why did you feel you had to make up a story?"

"What do you mean?"

"I met Veronique on her way to her piano lesson. She was very pleased because you had been home for lunch today!"

So that was it! Since he had arrived to pick her up for dinner, Mireille had been waiting for an explanation he hadn't even thought of giving her. Instead of coming out with it right off the bat, she had chosen to sulk like a little girl. She reminded him of Veronique! Yet he was touched, somehow, especially when she added in a hurt tone, "Did your client cancel at the last minute?"

"No. It was silly of me not to tell you. Aunt Elise called and asked me to come home."

"Knowing your aunt, I can well understand why you'd drop everything and run!"

"One up for you, Mireille!" Pierre pretended to mark a score in the air.

"If she wanted you to drop everything and go right home, it must have been something important."

"Yes, I guess you could say that. She'd made a commitment to see some contractor about a painting job."

He couldn't help it; no sooner did he start to tell her

the truth than he felt the need to come up with another lie! And he could have easily gone on in this vein, but he wanted her forgiveness right away.

"I took advantage of the situation to take you out to dinner and have you to myself for longer. . . . "

She hesitated before speaking. "You're telling me the truth?"

"I told you this morning on the phone: I thought we should elope immediately! Who ever heard of eloping in broad daylight?"

"Oh, Pierre . . . ! Well, you're forgiven. Now I can tell you that the change in plans suited me perfectly. For lunch, we'd be just two friends meeting; but for dinner, the whole atmosphere is different, more intimate. . . . Don't you agree?"

He lowered his head and took the hand she was offering across the table. It excited him to hold this tender hand and feel it tremble in his, to be so close to her smiling face. The maître d', who was on his way to their table, suddenly headed in a different direction.

"You are ravishing, Mireille. Every time I'm with you, I wonder if perhaps you'd rather be with someone else."

The young woman threw him a look of surprise.

"Why do you say that? Do I look bored when I'm with you?"

"Well, not exactly—let's forget tonight because you were angry with me—but you have to admit that sometimes you just put up with me, pretend to be interested in what I'm talking about. I just can't help thinking you'd have a much better time with young people, or at least a younger man. . . . "

"Keep talking like that and I'll really get angry!"

"Then let's change the subject. I want to see you smile: it's what I like best in all the world!"

She laughed joyfully. Pierre, however, was not too

pleased with his remark; although it had been gallant, he considered it rather gauche. Suddenly, thinking that Doctor Guillou might be observing their little tête-à-tête, he pulled his hand away.

The maître d' brought the champagne he had placed in an ice-bucket just a few minutes earlier.

From then on, the conversation was lighthearted and bubbly, just like the wine in their glasses.

Mireille kept the conversation simple and lively by making comments about their mutual friends. Whenever there was a lull, Pierre would tell a story, and they would both laugh.

Once again, he felt young, wanting only to be happy and have fun. He didn't even think about Aunt Elise's comments, Farges's theories and the mysterious Sea Gull.

Until the letter arrived.

It was time for dessert. Mireille was savoring a banana flambé. Pierre was watching her admiringly, saying whatever came into his head just for the pleasure of hearing her laugh.

Only aware of themselves, they hadn't noticed the maître d' looking in their direction, whispering to the doorman.

Finally, the doorman approached their table, carrying a small silver tray.

"Pardon me. Mademoiselle Farges? I have a letter for you that has just been delivered."

Mireille burst out laughing. "Well, now I've seen everything! A letter for me? In a restaurant?"

"Probably one of your admirers," said Pierre, amused, "There are any number of them in here tonight!"

The doorman handed her the tray. On it was a plain white envelope

Pierre frowned and his tone of voice changed.

"May I? I'd like to look at the envelope, just for a second."

As soon as he saw it, his face fell. He suddenly remembered the letter Elise had received; he was positive the name had been typed on the same old typewriter.

The setup was identical: the name typed low on the envelope, and up on the left, the notation, "Personal" underlined twice.

"Who gave you this letter?" Pierre asked the man.

"I don't know."

"What do you mean, you don't know?"

"I'm sorry, monsieur, I don't know. No new guests were coming in, and I left the door to help in the wine cellar. I found the letter on my desk when I returned to the lobby. This note was attached to it. . . ."

It was a standard sheet of paper, folded in two, and read, "To be delivered to the table reserved by M. Lalonde."

"That will be all, thank you."

Pierre turned around and casually surveyed the room. No one seemed to have noticed the incident. The babble of voices had become progressively louder during the meal; subdued conversations had given way to louder talk and more laughter. The atmosphere at Doctor Guillou's table seemed very relaxed and happy. Only one old couple, probably strangers to the area, were eating quietly.

"What is this?" demanded Mireille. "You look like you don't want to give me the letter. Give it to me. I'm dying to know what's in it!"

Pierre made no move to surrender it. Troubled, he only stared at Mireille. Still laughing, she added, "I see. You're jealous! You think it's a love letter."

He decided to go along with that.

"Maybe it is and maybe it isn't. I'm not sure I want to risk it!"

"What risk?"

"Having to compete with a younger rival."

"Do you really think it would change anything? You don't have much faith in me."

"Let's just say I know how fickle a young woman can be."

"Just watch it, or I'm going to get angry!" Then she implored him. "Come on, Pierre. Be a good sport and give me the letter! I promise to let you read it after."

"Why don't you finish your dessert first?"

Once more, Pierre turned around to look at the others in the room. His eyes met only those of Doctor Guillou. He really couldn't make out his expression, because the doctor quickly turned away.

He had to think fast! The champagne wasn't helping any . . . . He knew there was a connection between this letter and the one Aunt Elise had received that morning, in the same mysterious way. It had to be from the Sea Gull. But why a letter to the daughter of his victim and not to Farges himself?

What should he do? Tear up the letter, rip it to tiny pieces? Mireille would be stunned at first, then furious; how could he justify such an action? Besides, it would only be a postponement. The Sea Gull would send another.

Mireille obviously was becoming annoyed at Pierre's strange behavior and beginning to wonder if this was still a game. She noticed Pierre's hand trembling as he held the letter; she was sure he wanted to destroy it. . . .

"Listen Mireille. . . . "

He hesitated, searching for the right words, knowing it was hopeless.

"I don't like the way this letter was sent to you. It might be better if you didn't read it."

Her reaction was precisely what he expected: she laughed.

"I don't believe this! Now my mail is being censored! You really are jealous!"

"No, just worried. I have a feeling this letter is bad news."

"Nonsense. It's just the wine making you sad. But it's doing exactly the opposite to me! Anyway there's only one way to find out who's right. . . . "

In a flash, she grabbed the letter from his hands and put it in her lap, out of his reach.

"Please, Mireille. . . . "

"You're so funny! Adam must have worn the same expression when Eve picked the apple! Do you really think I shouldn't read this letter when it's addressed to me?"

"That's exactly what I think. I'm only trying to protect you. . . . "

"From what? At least you could wait until you found out who wrote it."

Pierre gave up. There was nothing more he could do. For the next few seconds, he could not take his eyes off Mireille's face. At first, she seemed surprised. She carefully commented that instead of a signature, the person had drawn a bird—a sea gull—and had typed out the word so there could be no mistake. . . .

Then her voice became oddly strained. "What does it mean?"

Her eyes hardened, her hands began to tremble. Pierre felt his anger growing; he could just imagine what was in the letter. . . .

Again the question came back. Why Mireille? Some sadistic quirk of character in the sender? To destroy Farges in the eyes of his own family before exposing him to the whole town? To cast doubt in the minds of the man's children? Could there be a more evil intent?

Pierre knew that he had been right: the Sea Gull was not interested in justice; these were the actions of an unbalanced person who would wind up doing more harm than good.

Mireille had finished reading. She was very pale as she slowly crumpled the letter in her hands.

Pierre didn't dare say anything; he knew that she was about to break down and cry. It would be disastrous here, among all these people.

He discreetly waved to the maître d'.

"Check please, quickly!"

Then, turning to Mireille, he told her he thought they should leave. A little fresh air would do them both good.

Without protest, she stood up and followed him like a small child. She waited in the lobby while he paid the check.

As he closed the door behind them, he sighed and took a deep breath of the misty night air. Street lights dotted the oceanside boulevard. On their left stood the old walls of the city, like some monstrous chunk of gray rubble tossed onto the shore by the waves.

"I forgot something. Sit in the car, Mireille. I'll be back in a second."

Thinking he probably shouldn't leave Mireille on her own without first having found out what the letter contained, he walked back to the restaurant. The letter couldn't have got there on its own. Someone had brought it, just like the one to his aunt!

The inside curtains on the glass door were not closed, and from the sidewalk, Pierre could see into the lobby that led to the dining room. Someone could easily have entered the lobby from outside without being seen.

The doorman was back at his post.

"I would like to have a word with the maître d'," said Pierre.

The man was with him in a second. Pierre pulled him aside and handed him some franc notes.

"I noticed that you were very alert and that your service was impeccable. I want you to think back and try to remember something."

The man was all ears.

"Do you recall if anyone left the room during dinner?"

"Of course, monsieur. That's easy; very few people did so. That older woman, sitting over there, came to get a sweater from the cloakroom."

"How long ago?"

"Quite a bit earlier on—it was not very warm when she first came in. Then, let's see, there was an English gentleman, who has already left; he came out to get some cigars. And Doctor Guillou. You know him, probably. He had to call the hospital in Quimper."

"How long ago was that?"

"Fifteen, maybe twenty minutes."

"Was the doorman on duty?"

"Ah . . . no, he wasn't. I had to show the doctor where the telephone was."

"Anyone else?"

"No one else. Pardon me, monsieur, but have you lost something?"

"No, and thank you very much. Forget all these questions. In fact, I never asked them."

"Consider it done, monsieur. You know, in my kind of work, my memory retains very little."

As he walked back to the car, Pierre was no closer to solving the mystery. He knew Guillou well: he was their family doctor. The man was a little older than Pierre, in good health, sports minded, a sailing enthusiast and a deep-sea fisherman. Somehow he didn't fit the picture of the Sea Gull.

Mireille was not crying, but her face seemed to have aged suddenly. She didn't move when Pierre slid across the seat closer to her. But when Pierre reached for her hand, she pulled away.

"Mireille . . . ?"

Surprised by her sudden movement, he looked at her inquiringly, stifling the urge to take her in his arms. She appeared to be in a daze.

"Don't pay any attention to that letter, " he said softly. "It's not meant to cause anything but trouble."

Mireille turned to look at him, her face cold and bitter. "How would you know?"

"I know. When someone draws a bird instead of signing his name —"

"You seemed to know what was in the letter even before it was opened."

"Not exactly. But it's a normal assumption, isn't it? Ordinary letters, letters on the up-and-up, arrive by mail."

"You seem to have it all figured out!"

"Why are you so defensive? Surely you don't think I had anything to do with it?"

Obstinately she didn't answer. Pierre thought she might be suffering from shock. This was not the time to get into a discussion. What Mireille needed now was sympathy and reassurance. When Pierre spoke, his voice was very gentle.

"It's probably just a very bad joke. Whatever it is, we'd better get to the bottom of it. Leave it to me. Mireille; show me the letter, no matter what it says. It can't be anything but a lot of nonsense."

"What if it's true?"

"Come now, truth has better ways of making itself known."

"Maybe it depends on what the truth is!"

"What do you mean?"

"You mean you really don't understand? You really don't know what's in this letter?"

"How could I know . . . ?"

"You don't know who sent it, either?"

He shrugged, completely puzzled and slightly annoyed. The girl's attitude did not fit the picture, as he saw it. He expected her to be indignant, to protest, but he hadn't expected her to turn on him. She was almost saying that he was the Sea Gull's accomplice . . . if not the Sea Gull himself!

It would have been very easy for him to straighten everything out. All he had to do was say that he knew the letter was meant to cause trouble even before she opened it. He could also guess what it said: probably much the same thing as his aunt's—allusion to certain facts, certain people. . . .

But his instinct told him to proceed slowly.

"It's up to you whether I read that letter or not; all I'm asking is that you believe me when I say I don't know where it came from or why it was sent."

As he spoke, he started the car, as if to suggest that the matter was closed. Mireille place her hand on his arm.

"Wait."

She opened her purse and took out the crumpled piece of paper.

"Here. After all, it concerns you as much as me."

"How's that?"

"Go ahead and read it. Maybe you can tell me why this . . . this Sea Gull seems to be so interested in our relationship! If you ask me, I'd say we're dealing with a female Sea Gull!"

Pierre turned on the interior light. From the very first line, his bewilderment grew from ordinary curiosity to sheer panic.

It would be a serious mistake to marry Pierre Lalonde—for both of you.
    You don't love him and he doesn't love you.

You are flattered to be seen with him because he's somebody; he likes to be seen with you because you are young and pretty. Marriage is not based on ego, but on true love.

A girl shouldn't choose a husband to please her parents.

As far as he's concerned, he only wants to marry again for practical reasons and because it seems the proper thing to do. Above all, he's looking for someone to take care of his children; you or someone else. Almost anyone else would be better; you hate children.

Your tastes are incompatible. After three weeks, you will be bored with each other; after three months, you will hate each other. Furthermore, his aunt will not leave the house and will probably do her best to make things worse.

Even when the odds are all on your side, marriage is still a risk. This one would be a catastrophe!

— The Sea Gull.

Chapter 5

Unaware that the evening would hold yet another, even greater surprise for him, Pierre drove Mireille home through the still streets.

He thought about the Sea Gull with some irritation, although this person, whoever he—or she—was, greatly intrigued him. The writer of the letters seemed to possess almost supernatural powers: the kind that can see into people's souls. . . .

How could he know the precise sequence of events that had happened four years previously; how could he know what was in Mireille's heart and in his own at that very moment? And what was his reason for this apparently objective interference? Did he consider it his mission to right what was wrong, to prevent further mistakes from occurring in the future?

For Mireille, it was all very simple: the Sea Gull was a woman, a rival, intent on having Pierre for herself.

Pierre smiled at the idea.

"I can't think of anyone who would fit that

description," he had said quite sincerely to Mireille, but she had remained unconvinced. During the drive back, she simply pouted, not saying a word. He should have told her that the Sea Gull was interested not only in their futures, but also in the past of elderly spinsters. . . .

No lights were on when he got home. Parking his car in the garage, he stood for a long time in front of the house, enjoying the sweet smell of fresh earth, recently turned up by the gardener.

For the first time, he was aware of spring. Was it the clear midnight sky, the softness of the warm breeze, or was it something new that stirred within him?

His feelings were mixed with sadness, as well—the kind of melancholy an adolescent feels while waiting anxiously for something, without knowing precisely what. In this state of mind, Pierre thought about Mireille: he was losing her, perhaps had already lost her. Or did he feel this way simply because he hadn't kissed her good night?

When he tried to take her into his arms, she pulled abruptly away and offered him her hand, explaining that she just couldn't get her mind off the letter.

There was nothing either of them could do about it. They would both remember, always, the words of the Sea Gull, and neither could deny the words were true.

" . . . You're flattered to be seen with him. . . . Above all, he wants someone to look after his children. . . . Your tastes are incompatible. . . . "

Every word expressed the absolute truth! How could they deny it? Mireille's intuition warned her right away: one minute they were happy together, the next, by the power of a few words, Pierre would not, could not, continue to be part of her future.

Pierre knew it, too; lies it seemed, were easier to take than the truth.

"You hate children. . . . "

Even had they not been true, those few words were enough to destroy his confidence in her capabilities to deal with Veronique and Michel. Anything she might say to the children, any attempts she might make to punish them, even if justified, would be suspect.

Pierre would always remember the letter and wonder about her feelings for the children. And they, with their uncanny intuition, would know how to take advantage of Mireille. The whole relationship would soon be hell.

The Sea Gull was diabolically clever! Because of those few words, Mireille would never be able to live with Pierre as his wife.

At last Pierre entered the house, took a bottle of mineral water from the refrigerator and climbed the stairs.

He chuckled to himself as he heard Elise's loud snoring: a sound that started low and ended in a whistle. Each time he heard it, he was surprised that such a small woman could make such a big noise!

The children slept peacefully in the next room; but then, they could sleep through anything. . . . Gently opening the door, Pierre peered at them in the light from the hallway.

Veronique was sleeping quietly, neatly covered by the blankets, the profile of her face delicately set against her soft golden hair. Her nose was snuggled against the head of the teddy bear that shared her pillow.

One leg dangling from the bed, all blankets on the floor, Michel appeared to have been dreaming of a boxing match. Whenever he slept, he looked like a warrior left for dead on the battlefield. Elise knew it and dressed him accordingly, making him wear woollen socks and a sweater over his pajamas. Every morning, he had to undress before he could get dressed.

With a burst of affection, Pierre tucked the blankets around his son. The boy lay still for a moment, muttering something in his sleep; then he flipped over, like a fish at the bottom of a boat, sending the blankets onto the floor, finally achieving a kneeling position in the bed, his rear raised high in the air.

Pierre smiled. Here, in the stillness of the dark room, he felt as though he were looking down at himself, so proud, yet so fragile. He was happy to have these two children but, at the same time, sad there wasn't a woman to share that happiness.

It was at such moments that the pain of being without Regine struck most sharply. Each time he stopped in to look at his sleeping children his memories became almost real, the past almost the present.

Regine would be there, quite suddenly, standing close to him, in her long, flowing nightgown. He could almost hear her breathe; she would reach for his hand, as if the joy was too great for her and she was about to faint. He would put his arm around her and they would walk together out of the room. . . .

But, in moments the fantasy would vanish, and Pierre would realize he was alone. And only the thought of his children made his misery bearable.

Pierre's mind returned to the present, to thoughts of Mireille. Strangely enough, he felt no regret. On the contrary, he felt free, almost relieved.

Had he actually seriously considered marrying her? Possibly. His ego had a lot to do with that, and he couldn't deny he found her attractive. But he couldn't picture her bending over the sleeping children, taking care of them, comforting them as a mother would. Would his infatuation with Mireille have been strong enough to overcome the problems?

At any rate, that possibility no longer existed, and Pierre felt grateful to the Sea Gull for forcing him to face reality. No matter how much he wanted female companionship, he did not have the right to expose his children to the risks of a bad marriage.

He covered the boy once more, almost without being aware of what he was doing. As he went to his room, he thought that maybe this would prove to be for the best. Perhaps he was meant to continue on his own. And from what the Sea Gull had said in Mireille's letter, he was sure he'd agree.

It didn't take Pierre long to realize his mistake. Searching for cigarettes in the pockets of his trench coat, he found a piece of paper. It was an envelope addressed to him, with the word "Personal" underlined twice. . . .

Quickly, he tore open the envelope and read the letter inside.

You are behaving like a college boy:
1. As far as your children are concerned:
You have taken the easy way out for yourself, but the worst possible way for them. Your Aunt Elise is an old shrew, decidedly not the woman to take their mother's place. She treats them well but is raising them badly: too strict, too sticky about rules, she is preventing them from growing up normally. What they need is someone younger, more aware of their needs, instead of an elderly spinster who considers discipline an end in itself.
2. As far as you're concerned:
Your relationship with Mireille Farges is absolutely meaningless. You would be making the worst mistake of your life to marry her! She is everything a woman and a mother should not be: silly, egotistical, small-minded. She would never accept the children

as her own and would make your whole life miserable.

Suggestion:
Go to Paris next week. Tuesday, at eleven o'clock,
go into the church of Saint-Germain-des-Prés. Kneel
in the seventh pew from the front to the left of the
main aisle. There, pray for happiness for yourself
and your children.

— The Sea Gull.

Chapter 6

In the harsh glare of the fluorescent light, the liquid took on the tones of a sapphire. But when the test tube was placed over the flame, the brilliant blue became dirty yellow, then gray, until at last the whole thing solidified.

Edward Perrelet turned off the Bunsen burner, put the test tube on its rack and the tongs on their shelf. He sat down and began neatly writing the results of the experiment in a notebook. He wrote these notes for every experiment: a daily, sometimes hourly, account.

Tall and slim, with brows slightly arched and white hair that grew down over the collar of his lab coat, he had the look of an elderly adolescent forgotten in the back of a classroom. His thick heavy glasses gave his blue eyes an air of innocence. When he put on his black coat, snug at the waist, he could have been on his way to play the organ in a dark church somewhere.

The workers had left almost an hour before. Only

Farges's office and the lab still showed a light. They occupied the same floor, directly across the central hallway from each other.

It was much the same every night. Perrelet was usually the last to go home, as if he was reluctant to leave his world of glass and metal, where multicolored chemical products stood on the shelves like strange flowers. He probably would have preferred to stay there all night, grabbing a quick bite to eat, then sleeping on a cot between two stills.

No one was waiting for him at home. Widowed for almost twenty years, he had no children; his only living relative was a brother in Venezuela with whom he no longer corresponded. A woman came in by day to look after his house and prepare his meals, at least on the days she was sober. If Perrelet came home and there was no meal ready, he would open a can or go to the small restaurant near the train station.

He appeared to have neither friends nor enemies. He talked very little and was a good listener, which explained why people thought him a sympathetic person. His co-workers found him too fussy, but they liked his even temperament and consistent politeness. Whether he was dealing with his boss or with an office boy, he was always the same: very polite and somewhat distant, which probably was due to indifference.

His only hobby was fishing. Every Sunday, no matter what the weather, he would put on his yellow raincoat and an old pair of pants, get behind the wheel of his old car and drive like a madman to the coast.

Anyone seeing him drive for the first time would never suspect he was on his way to the sea for a leisurely day of fishing. It was much more likely they would think he was in a rally, or playing a part in an old gangster movie. . . . Acquaintances were always surprised when they saw him tearing by, for his driving was so unlike everything else he did; actually, it was in total opposition to the rest of his behavior. But he was considered a genius and his eccentricities were, therefore, permissible.

Steps were heard in the hallway and Farges's silhouette appeared against the translucent window of the lab door. This was the only room where he stopped to knock before entering.

This late visit had become a tradition. Farges never left the plant without stopping for a few words with his chemist, the only employee for whom he had any real consideration and respect.

"So, where are we with the new tests?"

"Just about where we were yesterday. . . . Excuse me, I'll be right with you."

Perrelet finished his notation, studied it a minute, then closed the book.

"We've had so many samples to analyze, I wasn't able to get back to the lotion until late this afternoon."

"That's not very good. You should be spending all your time in research!"

Farges began to walk between the counters. He took out his cigarette case, then put it back in his pocket, remembering that smoking was forbidden in the lab.

"In our field," he went on, "we must constantly be developing new products. Most of our customers are women; they are forever changing their minds; yet they are easily led. We can sell them anything tomorrow as long as it's not the same thing we sold them today. It isn't by analyzing products that we'll come up with new ones. Leave that to the other workers!"

"They just don't seem to be able to handle it."

"Because there's too much work or because they're not good enough?"

"Because there's too much to do."

"Then hire more people, for God's sake! I've told you that a hundred times."

"Until now, it hasn't been necessary, I've been able to keep up by coming in early in the morning and staying a few hours at night. . . ."

"I know, Perrelet, I know; you've never been a clock watcher. But that isn't the point. I don't want you to waste time on things any new employee could do just as well."

"If we hire another person, it should be someone to assist me in my research."

Farges stopped dead in his tracks.

"Well, that's a new twist. Until now, you've always wanted to be the only one doing research."

"I've been thinking about that; I've decided that I have no right to continue thinking this way. I have to look ahead to the day I'll retire."

"You're not thinking of quitting, are you?"

"I'm over sixty, Monsieur Farges."

"So what? You're in top shape. I've never known you to miss a day."

"No one is immune to sickness or accident forever. If something should happen to me . . . ."

"I've thought about that, too, but what's the rush? There'll be time enough to do something about it when you have to be off for one reason or other."

"Who's going to check out the person who'd have to replace me? Who'd show him the way we do things?"

"What is all this? What's come over you, Perrelet? You're talking as though you were leaving tonight!"

The chemist smiled.

"Don't worry. I have no intention of leaving tonight. It hasn't even entered my mind. But I must say that if I were you, considering how important research is to this company . . . ."

As he spoke, he took off his white coat, hung it in

the closet near the door and returned to the desk where he began straightening out his papers.

"There's no point in starting on something new tonight," he muttered regretfully.

Farges, frowning, did not want to appear to be hanging over the other man's shoulder.

"You see, Perrelet, I'd be a little uneasy if you were to hire an assistant. You would be, too, for that matter. You like things quiet, and you're used to working alone. I can't see you giving instructions to somebody who'd be trying to tell you what to do two days later!"

"Don't misunderstand me. I'm not suggesting this for my own sake."

"And another thing: anyone hired as your assistant, would have to have his degree as a pharmacist or a chemist and would have to be paid accordingly."

Perrelet shrugged his shoulders at the obvious conclusion.

"And there's one more serious objection," continued Farges. "What about the risk of leaks? I have no intention of allowing our formulas and manufacturing processes to get into the hands of our competitors."

"That's a risk you'll have to take sooner or later."

"Not necessarily. If I found someone who would be part of the business . . . ."

Perrelet remained silent for a moment, then asked if Farges were referring to his son.

"Yes. I know what you're thinking: he doesn't seem to be heading that way. But I refuse to give up; he will get his bachelor's degree!"

"I wonder if it's a good thing for his whole life to be locked up in chemistry, when he really hates—"

"Right now, he hates everything that requires an effort, no matter what it is! We'll see. If he can't handle it, I'll find a place for him in the commercial end of the business, but I want to try everything I can, first. That's why I'd like things to stay the way they are for a few years, at least."

Perrelet did not answer. He was busy tidying up the top of his desk, like a schoolboy at the end of a lesson: pencils in one drawer, notes and books in another.

Once more, Farges's voice distracted him.

"Have you seen this? There's a letter for you here on the table."

Farges was ready to go, but his curiosity kept him from leaving the room.

"And a personal letter at that! It must be from the accounting department. That poor accountant is terrified of being indiscreet—he'd do the same thing if it was only junk mail."

Perrelet crossed quickly to the table. "Strange," he murmured, "that letter wasn't there a minute ago, when the girls left . . . and nobody has come in here except you. . . ."

Farges began to laugh.

"Well, I certainly didn't bring it in! You must have been concentrating on an experiment and didn't notice the door open. It was probably Gerald on his way out —"

Farges stopped, struck by the change that had come over Perrelet, who had torn open the envelope and had started to read the letter. His quiet face had become tense. The difference was so noticeable that Farges moved a step closer to him.

He had just enough time to see what appeared to be a drawing of a bird at the bottom of the page.

Perrelet suddenly sat down in a chair. He shoved the paper into his pocket and tried to force a smile. He realized that Farges was staring at him in surprise.

"It's . . . it's nothing important," he mumbled. "Someone in the office apparently is trying to play a joke on me. I . . . I'm happy to think that anyone would take the trouble. . . . "

Farges did not seem convinced. "Personally," he grumbled, annoyed, "I don't like this very much! I'm not paying people to play games around here!"

Perrelet glanced at the calendar hanging on the wall next to his desk.

"Once a year, you have to expect a little foolishness; today is April the first. . . . "

Then he picked up the envelope he had left on the table.

"Anyway, look at the envelope. It wasn't typed in this office—we don't have a typewriter this old."

Farges did not answer. He was expecting Perrelet to show him the letter, which would have put an end to the whole incident.

But the chemist seemed to have forgotten it. As though nothing had happened, he walked back to his desk and resumed the task of tidying up his papers.

Farges looked at the man for almost a full minute. Perrelet always upset him, but tonight, his behavior bothered him even more. He felt that Perrelet was lying to him, or at the very least, that he was keeping something from him.

If it was just a prank, why had he looked so surprised and worried as he was reading the letter? Was it as innocent as he was trying to pretend? In any case, it must have come from inside the plant: there was no address or stamp on it.

The president of a large company can't know everything that goes on in his factory, but he hates to be faced with proof that something was put over on him. That was what Farges found most disturbing: feeling that his employees, including his closest associate, were involved in something together behind his back, perhaps even plotting against him!

Seeing that Perrelet was busy at his desk as though he had completely forgotten he was there, Farges said a very abrupt good night and left.

Once the door was closed, Perrelet took the letter from his pocket and spread it on his desk. There was a strange expression on his face: he looked very serious, though a sparkle of amusement danced in his eyes.

Yet, what was in the letter would not appear to give him any reason to rejoice.

Edward Perrelet, you are a coward.

You have been working for a swindler for the past four years. All this time, you have been his accomplice.

So as not to upset your life-style, you continue to endure the worst injustices. Mme Lachenaire was counting on your support, but you betrayed her confidence in you.

Her children gave you their affection, but you left them destitute.

There is still time to save yourself, to do something about it. You need an assistant. George Lachenaire will soon complete his pharmaceutical studies. He must take his rightful place in the company.

It's up to you.

—The Sea Gull.

Chapter 7

" . . . Seventh pew to the left off the center aisle : . . ."

Pierre checked again to make sure he had not made any mistake. It was five after eleven. The Sea Gull's "suggestion" had been followed precisely to the minute. Nothing. Nothing was happening. Did he really hope something would?

In front of him, to the right, he saw the silhouette of a woman in black. The white splash of a surplice appeared and as quickly disappeared into a confessional. The sliding wooden panel of the confessional was heard. The slightest noise seemed exaggerated and prolonged; one had the impression of being inside a large stone shell. The sexton quietly went about his duties, dusting the pews.

Pierre was kneeling, his face buried in his hands. His eyes were still heavy with sleep. His trip had not been too pleasant; he had been unable to relax. The sleeping car of the train had been very hot and he had slept very little by the time the train had pulled into the Montparnasse station at daybreak.

The most annoying part, perhaps, was Pierre's impatience with himself. He had the feeling that he was doing something absolutely absurd, following the instructions of a "sea gull" like a child obeying his parents.

He realized how ridiculous the situation was. Here he was, the busy president of a large industry, leaving his responsibilities behind to come to Paris for no reason whatsoever! Normally a rational man, here he was in a church a long way from home, waiting for he knew not what, on the orders of a stranger who was either a joker or a maniac!

Pierre tried to justify his behavior: he had followed the Sea Gull's instructions because he was still young and open to adventure. Something from his youth was still alive in him: a certain compulsion to explore the unknown. . . .

And in order to discover the identity of the Sea Gull, didn't he have to "play the game"?

Contrary to Pierre's first impression, the Sea Gull was not typical of most anonymous-letter writers. He was not exposing hidden facts; he was bringing to light people's feelings. He was playing the role of each person's conscience, and a perceptive conscience at that! He was bringing out in the open the embarrassing thoughts that people, through cowardice, would rather keep hidden.

For Elise, it was knowing that Farges robbed the Lachenaire family of their rightful ownership of the business, then living with the remorse that had resulted from having done nothing to make things right. For Mireille and Pierre, it was their lack of love for each other and the incompatibilities that would make marriage a serious mistake.

" . . . Pray for happiness for yourself and your children. . . . "

Pierre recalled the prayers of his youth and tried to put full meaning into them, but his thoughts strayed. Instead, in his mind's eye, appeared the accusations made by the Sea Gull.

" . . . Your aunt is not raising your children properly. . . . She's preventing them from growing normally. . . ."

For four days now, Pierre hadn't been able to put the letter out of his mind. The truth in it made him very uncomfortable. He knew very well that his aunt had very few maternal instincts and was raising Veronique and Michel according to principles outdated fifty years ago!

What could be done? For anyone not involved, it was easy to criticize and say that this or that should be done. . . .

"They need someone young and more capable of seeing to their needs. . . . "

Of course! Someone who could get along with Aunt Elise and at the same time be able to override her decisions; in other words, a person who could perform miracles!

Maybe that's why the Sea Gull had sent Pierre to this church, to pray for a miracle! Or was it merely to test his power over people? If that were the case, the Sea Gull might be somewhere in the church, watching his "puppet"!

The minutes crept by: eleven-fifteen . . . eleven-twenty. . . . The black silhouettes slipped in and out of the confessional. A priest, preceded by an altar boy, went down the center aisle to perform a baptism. From the side of the church the happy murmuring of the family could be heard, accompanied from time to time by whimpers from the baby.

Pierre decided to wait until eleven-thirty. As the time went by, he became more and more puzzled. He had a vague feeling of anticipation. Perhaps a second letter, with more concrete suggestions as to what to do about the children?

The situation was becoming too much! Pierre had given up trying to justify his actions, but he couldn't help smiling at his foolishness. His curiosity was not the only thing involved. His desire to find out the identity of the Sea Gull was normal, but there was something else: something inherited from his Breton ancestors. He had a taste for mystery, for magic, for anything that appeared to defy the laws of nature and reason.

Eleven twenty-five . . . eleven twenty-seven. . . . Pierre suddenly became aware of someone discreetly approaching his pew . . . kneeling close by. First, he noticed blond hair against the collar of a gray coat; then a delicate hand . . . no wedding ring.

It must be more than coincidence. The place was almost deserted; why would a young woman have chosen this pew?

Pierre was unable to see her face, but something else was much more bewildering. The way she moved, the color of her hair, jolted a hidden recess in his memory. Something from the past . . . .

She finally turned her head and their eyes met. Identical expressions of astonishment came over their faces. Simultaneously, they spoke.

"Pierre!"

"Françoise!"

Françoise Lachenaire. Pierre had not seen her since the death of her father, since the time he had held her hand for a long moment at the gates of the cemetery. He remembered the small, weeping figure, the tears that sparkled through the black veil. . . .

Through his startled and confused thoughts, he tried to guess the reason for this strange meeting. It was no use; he simply couldn't think straight. The emotions he was feeling at seeing Françoise again were overwhelming.

"We can't talk here," he whispered. "Can we leave?"

She agreed, but remained kneeling for a few more minutes, her head bowed and her hands joined in prayer. Pierre leaned slightly back to study her and thought about his strange impression of a moment ago before she'd turned her head. . . .

A few years earlier, just before Regine's death, he had shared a pew with Françoise in the church at Quimper. They had often run into each other, but on that particular day he had been struck by the beauty of her face and the glow of her hair. He had felt as though he were seeing her face for the first time. Previously he had always thought of her as a child, but he remembered mentioning to Regine that one day Françoise would grow into a beautiful woman.

Well, today, she was a woman and, indeed, quite beautiful. And it was not chance that had brought them together. . . .

As they were leaving the church, Pierre had a strange feeling. His eyes sought out the shadowy figures standing at the back of the church. He noticed a tall, young man, wearing glasses, turn and walk away. Pierre was reminded of George Lachenaire, Françoise's brother. But it was no more than a fleeting impression and might have been brought on by his seeing Françoise.

Once outside, they stopped for a moment and looked at each other as though to make sure they had not been mistaken. The noise, the crowd, the traffic, assured them that it was all very real.

"What shall we do?" asked Pierre. "We have two choices: we can go have a coffee or simply look straight ahead and start walking. Of course, we could also stay right here, but in the middle of Paris, it's not easy to stand still!"

"I'd like to walk," she answered.

"Good! I spent all night on the train, and I have to convince myself that I'm not sleeping . . . that this is not all a dream," he added with a smile.

They walked along Boulevard Saint-Germain-des-Prés toward the Odeon. The cloudy day still had the feel of winter, despite the tiny buds beginning to sprout on the branches.

For a long while, they did not speak. Pierre could not find the right words to start a conversation. Too many questions were going through his head. He finally decided to set aside everything else, for the time being, and simply express what he was feeling.

"I'm sorry, Françoise. I'm not very talkative. You must think I'm either stupid or very rude. Actually, I'm still in a state of shock at having met you this way!"

"Really?"

She was smiling, but her eyes were bewildered. Pierre had the feeling she didn't believe him.

"You don't seem too convinced, but honestly, I mean it. Tell me, instead, how you feel about meeting me?" he asked her. "Or, did you know I'd be in the church?"

"No. I waited quite a while before I knelt beside you. I didn't recognize you, at first."

"So that's why I had to wait so long! I was there at eleven, just like the letter said. I was just about ready to give up, when you arrived."

"A letter? What did you say about a letter?"

"From our mutual friend, the Sea Gull. You, too, right?"

To answer his question, the young woman opened her bag and took out an envelope. It had all of the characteristics Pierre had come to recognize, with an important difference: it was addressed and stamped.

"It arrived Friday morning," said Françoise. "No

need to tell you I haven't stopped asking myself a whole lot of questions since!"

"Was it sent from Quimper?"

"From Douarnenez."

Pierre stopped to examine the postmark.

"Strange. It proves that the Sea Gull is not in this area. It was mailed Thursday, apparently in the afternoon; the postmark shows the time of the last pickup. But I received my letter the same night in Concarneau, but in a much more original way. While I was having dinner in a restaurant, the Sea Gull slipped it into the pocket of my trench coat in the car!"

Pierre took his letter out of his attaché case.

"Here it is. As you can see, both letters were typed on the same machine, and have the same signature."

"And no doubt, they give the same instructions?"

The letter Françoise handed to Pierre contained only four typed lines.

Next Tuesday, go into the Saint-Germain-des-Prés church at eleven o'clock. Kneel in the seventh pew on the left and pray for happiness for yourself and your family.

—The Sea Gull

Pierre handed the letter back to her.

"The instructions in mine are identical, almost word for word," he said, as he folded the letter and showed her the "suggestion" at the bottom of his letter.

"But for me," he said, "this invitation, if we can call it that, follows a great deal of criticism and reproach. The Sea Gull is not at all happy with the way I run my life. And he doesn't beat around the bush telling me what he thinks! It's been a long time since anyone has raked me over the coals like that.

"Forgive me for not letting you read it," he said as he put it back in his case. "What it has to say would be of little interest to you and is anything but flattering to me, as well as a few other people we know!"

Neither spoke as they continued to stroll through the crowd they did not even notice. Françoise still had a strange smile on her lips.

Pierre was immersed in thought. This walk was taking him back six years to a previous time he had walked beside this young girl. . . .

It was summertime, and they met almost every evening to play tennis: Regine and Pierre on one side; Françoise and her brother, George, on the other. Despite the differences in their ages, they had good times together. After the game, they would relax at a café along the banks of the Odet.

At that time, Françoise must have been sixteen or seventeen. Regine would tease her husband, saying that the young girl had a crush on him.

Happy times that death had put to an end. Françoise and Pierre had suffered, fought and matured, during a time when they had been far apart from each other. And now, they had been reunited by most unusual circumstances.

They exchanged few words as they continued their stroll toward the Seine. But each time they looked at each other, when the crush of the crowd caused them to brush against each other, a kind of happiness glowed in their eyes.

When they reached the banks of the river Seine, Pierre took her arm.

"The Seine is very different from the Odet," he said. "Yet, I have the feeling that we've done all this before. How should I put it . . . ? The past seems to have come to life again. For you, of course, it must be different.

You were so young when we used to play tennis!
You've probably forgotten all about those days!"

"Forgotten? If you only knew. . . . "

Pierre held onto her arm. Before them stood the gray
backdrop of Notre-Dame, silhouetted against the dull
sky.

"Those were the last happy moments I can
remember," continued Françoise. "For four years now,
I've thought about them almost constantly."

"Forgive me. I thought . . . ." Unable to find the
words to express his feelings, Pierre did not finish his
sentence. He felt very sad: he had been the one who
had forgotten their friendship. How often had he even
thought about what had happened to the Lachenaire
family after Maurice's death?

"At that time," he added, "I must have seemed like
an old man to you!"

"An old man of thirty-three. See, I remember exactly
how old you were." She looked at him and smiled.
"You're right, of course. But now, you seem much
younger. You don't intimidate me nearly as much as
you used to!"

"With me, it's the opposite; I still feel older, but now
you intimidate me! I remember you as a child, and now
I see before me a young woman. But something mysterious has been added that tells me to be wary."

She laughed in amazement. "I've never been told
anything like that before!"

"What I'm trying to say is that a man of my age has
to be careful of youth and beauty."

"Why? You don't strike me as that type."

He made a vague gesture in the air. Françoise was
right: usually he paid little attention to how he impressed other people or their effect on him, least of all,
young women. With Mireille, the idea had never occurred to him. But now. . . .

What he was feeling was not insecurity or shyness; it was more the feeling that he was living a very important chapter in his life. From the very moment he had met Françoise's eyes, he had felt something stir deep inside, something that gave new meaning to every motion, every word. A kind of spell . . . infatuation . . . or, perhaps, it was only the strangeness of the situation. . . .

His thoughts had come full circle. He was back to the mysterious Sea Gull.

"This is just like a fairy tale," he said, "a world totally unfamiliar to me. I'm normally a very practical man, a man who works with forecasts, balance sheets, cause and effect. . . . The letters I receive are almost never signed by birds. . . . "

"Neither are mine!"

"Are you asking yourself the same questions as I am?"

"Who is the Sea Gull and why did he arrange this meeting?"

"Exactly! Since last Thursday, I've gone over all my friends, all the people I know. I've told myself it could be so and so . . . this one, or that one . . . but I can't be sure. Every time I make a hypothesis, it doesn't hold up. Besides . . . . "

He hesitated, seeing the question in Françoise's eyes.

"Besides, the Sea Gull is interested in other people too. At least two others have received letters, signed the same way ours were."

"In Quimper?"

"Yes, and I've read them both. There doesn't seem to be any connection between the two, except that the people who received them know each other. In one case, the Sea Gull seems to want to bring justice; in another, he's trying to be a kind of genie. He issues orders as well as advice: 'Do this! Don't do that!' And so far, he seems to be right all the way. His letter to me is proof enough that he knows a great deal about my life and my problems."

He leaned toward Françoise and added, "The letter also shows that the Sea Gull wants to help me. I'm grateful to him for having brought us together. It was so simple, yet might never have happened if it hadn't been for the letter!"

She turned to look at him, and there was a smile on her face. She seemed to have smiled a lot in the short while they had been together. This time, their eyes met and clung. Pierre stopped walking.

"Listen to me, Françoise. I don't think I expressed myself too well just then. I may have sounded as though I was only trying to be polite, but I want you to know I'm very happy to have found you again."

"I feel the same way, Pierre."

She had stopped smiling and her face had become serious. Yet, she still seemed surprised. Her green eyes had darkened yet were more radiant then before . . . like the depths of the ocean, where sunlight becomes soft amber.

He could see her as she had been many years before. She had changed very little; she had simply become more delicate, somehow, now that she was aware of her womanhood. She seemed extremely vulnerable, a quality Pierre found appealing.

He knew that the scene before him would stay forever in his mind. The fine spring mist, the people in the streets, the sidewalk book stalls, the budding trees along the river, the boats gliding on the glistening water and most of all this face so close to him. . . .

"Will you have lunch with me?" he asked. "There's so much to talk about!"

"I'll have to call home."

"And what about the rest of the afternoon?"

"I have no lessons until six o'clock."

"No other obligations, no appointments? Marvelous! That Sea Gull is something else, isn't he? He knew your schedule too. Here we are with lots of time to get to know each other all over again . . . because we're not the same people, you know; we're both quite different from the memory we have of each other. . . . Let's walk to Île Saint-Louis. I love that part of Paris!"

"You, too? When we first moved here, I wanted to live there. Being a simple country girl, I thought it would be so easy. . . . "

"Like many things, it's only easy when you have lots of money."

"Well, we didn't. We were very lucky to find the apartment we are living in now; I guess you can't have everything."

The noonday crowd along the river had grown larger. Some people strolled among the book stalls and paintings while others were rushing to do their shopping before going back to work. The pace was almost frantic. Constantly jostled by the crowd Pierre and Françoise found conversation very difficult.

Once they had crossed the river, they were in the country again, where the narrow old streets were peaceful and quiet.

"I know a very nice restaurant farther along the river. Let's have lunch there. With a little luck, we can get a table with a view of the Seine."

Luck was with them. Sitting in a corner, close to the window, they could see between the trees to the boat traffic on the river. A loud blast of a boat whistle seemed to change the whole atmosphere.

"Here we are in Brittany again . . . " whispered Françoise.

Pierre was reminded of a few days earlier, when he and Mireille had dinner together. The similarity between the two events struck him. He almost expected the waiter to come over to the table and hand Françoise a letter from the Sea Gull.

But there was no letter, though the presence of the invisible Sea Gull was very much with them throughout the meal.

Chapter 8

"Veronique," Pierre was saying, "although she is quite delicate, is very much her own person. She's most refined . . . almost too much so, sometimes. She makes me feel clumsy, somehow, because she seems so dainty. But with Michel, I'm much more at ease; we get along great together. Mind you, that doesn't stop us from having some pretty wild arguments. Even Aunt Elise stays out of it when we get going. . . ."

Françoise was laughing, and Pierre loved the way she looked when she was enjoying herself and the way she listened to his every word. The glow in her eyes when he spoke of the children warmed his heart.

It was time for coffee and cigarettes, and the waiters were busy with the few remaining customers. Outside, the sun had broken through the clouds, and the day had become warmer. Everything seemed more beautiful.

"The sun will be out completely soon. Let's go for a

walk on Île Saint-Louis!" Pierre suggested enthusiastically.

He was relaxed as if he was on holiday; he had forgotten what it was like to be carefree, and it took him a long time to realize he was really happy. Happy to be with this young woman, to see her smile, to share the emotions reflected in her face and voice.

For the first time in many years, he was interested in someone besides his children.

"Françoise, I'm going to ask you a question—a silly question, perhaps, but very important. You'll understand in a minute. . . . "

She waited, a little worried by his serious tone and the anxiety in his eyes.

"Are you happy living in Paris?"

"Happy? Since we moved here, I haven't really been living; it's been more like surviving, fighting against something that is trying to destroy me!"

"How so?

"I feel like a prisoner, locked away from everything I love: the open fields, the wind, the sea . . . especially the sea! When I'm in the subway, I feel terrible, because I know there are vast beaches where I could be walking without seeing anything but the water and the sky!"

"I know what you mean, I'm sure I'd feel the same way."

"It's impossible to get used to Paris after growing up in a place like Brittany."

"Why not say, 'when we love what deserves to be loved. . . . ' It doesn't happen too often. I'm sure that a lot of young women in Quimper would be delighted to change places with you." *Especially,* he thought, *Mireille, who only dreams of cocktails and fashionable restaurants.*

"The worst part of it all is that we don't really have to live in Paris. Mother decided to make the move, pretending that George could go to better schools here. As if he couldn't study to become a pharmacist in Brittany!"

Pierre recalled his aunt's words of several days earlier. "In Quimper, she would have been very unhappy not to have been able to go on living the way she was used to."

Françoise gave him a surprised look.

"How unusual for a man to think that way. . . . "

Pierre felt a twinge of guilt but didn't bother to explain that he hadn't really been speaking his own thoughts.

"You're right, of course," continued the young woman, "she would have been miserable. I guess that's what bothers me most, this business of giving such monumental importance to things that really don't matter."

"You're being rather hard on your mother."

"I'm just sorry to see her making such a mess of her life, as well as her children's. Please don't misunderstand me, Pierre, I'm not blaming her for the mistakes she made when father died. . . . I guess you know what happened?"

"My aunt mentioned it the other day. She was telling me that Farges. . . . "

"Yes, my mother has paid dearly for her confidence in that man, but under the circumstances, she could hardly be expected to do anything else. She had no way of knowing that he would take advantage of the situation to take over the business and throw us out! He was so slick that no one knew what was happening until it was done."

Pierre immediately thought about the Sea Gull; he knew what Farges had done! He hesitated. Was this the right time to say something to Françoise about the letter his aunt had received?

Without really knowing why—perhaps because he didn't want to risk spoiling the good time they were having—he decided to wait. Instead, he spoke of something else.

"In any case, nobody stays interested very long in other people's affairs. I hope now that four years have gone by, your mother has got over—"

"After four years, she's exactly where she was the first day! She rehashes regrets and useless grudges. When she thinks about George, she becomes very upset. He should have inherited the laboratory, but the way things are, it will be years before he'll be able to afford his own pharmacy!"

"You can't blame her for being upset about that."

"But why stay angry at a situation you can't change? And why blame someone else for your own misery? Mother has a right to hate Farges; but she also hates everyone who stayed on with him after my father died. Like poor old Perrelet . . . do you know him?"

"Vaguely. I see him once in a while. He reminds me of some mad professor."

"Mother is convinced he could have protected our interests, but he preferred to work for Farges."

"My aunt never told me anything about him, but I have a feeling she also thinks along those lines."

"Come now! Perrelet didn't know what was going on. He's quite oblivious to everything around him . . . but you mentioned your aunt. She certainly deserves every respect from our family. She resigned the day of the funeral."

"She liked your father very much but never could stand Farges. On the other hand, without trying to make her seem undeserving of your mother's more benevolent feelings, I should tell you that she worked mainly for her own pleasure. It's very easy to make that kind of noble gesture when you don't have to worry about earning a living. That was when she moved in with me. I was having a rather difficult time at the house. . . . "

There was a silence for a moment while their eyes followed a red and black boat, piloted by a lone man, standing very erect at the wheel.

"What does your brother think of all this?"

"With me, he's a friend. With mother, he's a typical affectionate son, looking after her as though she were ailing and unable to care for herself."

"I suppose he agrees with her? It must be very hard for him to accept being pushed out of a business he should have inherited."

"Of course it is. Especially since he was brought up with the idea of following in father's footsteps. George keeps very much to himself. He never shows what he feels, and he's strong-willed. He works hard, always keeps his distance . . . . "

"You get along well together?"

"Yes, but we're not particularly close; we never really get involved in each other's life. For example, he is corresponding with a girl from Quimper, one of my childhood friends, and I think he loves her very much. But he never mentions a word to me about it. He knows I'm aware of it because I handle the mail."

"Does he confide in your mother?"

"Even less than he does with me, if that's possible! He never contradicts her, never expresses his feelings. She doesn't seem to notice it; as long as someone keeps listening to her . . . . "

"By the way, did you show them the letter from the Sea Gull?"

"Only George knows about it. Thank God, mother wasn't there when it arrived. She's a chronic worrier, and if she'd seen it, she'd have had a fit!"

"How did your brother react?"

"He simply told me not to mention it to mother. He said it probably was just a joke, but that I should be careful of anonymous letters. At any rate, he accompanied me to the church. . . . Why are you smiling?"

"Because I was right! I thought I recognized George at the back of the church, when we were leaving."

"And you didn't say anything!"

"I wasn't positive. I haven't seen him for a long time."

"Well, I guess he's not worried about you."

"What does that mean?"

"We agreed that he would step in if he felt there was something wrong. He must have been reassured when he recognized you. And I was so surprised to see you, I completely forgot about George!"

Françoise started to laugh.

"He'll be wondering all day what this meeting is all about. But I know if I decide not to say a word tonight, he won't ask me anything."

"Tell him about it, Françoise, and tell your mother, too. Tell them I'll be waiting for you to come to Quimper, as soon as you can get away."

"That you . . . that you'll be waiting for me?"

"To look after my children. You do give private lessons, don't you? Believe me, they could both use them!"

"But, Pierre—"

"Orders of the Sea Gull; the matter needs no discussion! Come, let's go outside; the sun is desperately trying to shine for us."

The patch of blue sky was growing bigger, and sunlight began to dance merrily on the waters of the Seine, as they left the restaurant.

They walked silently to the tip of the island and leaned against the sunlit breastwork.

"Look, Françoise, our ship is ready to set sail. The

city hall, the Saint-Jacques tower, all these images in stone will disappear in the distance . . . we will travel down the Seine to the ocean. How long will it take us to reach Quimper if we sail up the Odet River?"

"Please, Pierre, don't make me feel any worse than I already do!"

"It's up to you. Listen, Françoise. The Sea Gull arranged our meeting not just so we'd spend only a few hours together. A little while ago, when I was talking about my children, I realized his intention. I don't know why I didn't think of it myself."

He took the letter out of his briefcase.

"First, the Sea Gull tells me: 'Your aunt is not raising your children properly. They need someone younger and more capable of understanding them.' Then a few lines later, he tells me how to go about finding you. He couldn't be much more direct than that, now, could he?"

Françoise did not answer. Her face was serious and her eyes were distant. The sun and the wind played in her hair.

"Here we are, thrown together by a stranger," Pierre continued, "and we both want to find out who it is. The best way to go about it is to follow his advice."

Françoise turned to look at him, her expression tense, almost hurt.

"It's impossible," she said.

"Let's give the Sea Gull the benefit of the doubt. Since he has suggested that solution, it's not only possible but very practical for both of us. He knows that, more than anything, you want to return to Brittany; he knows that my children are not being raised properly. So, he's showing us a simple way of righting the situation."

"Very simple, if you can ignore all the obstacles. My mother, for one."

"Didn't I understand you to suggest that you and your mother aren't exactly on the best of terms?"

"That's true. Mother isn't the easiest person in the world to live with, and sometimes she upsets me. But then, it works both ways. I try not to show my feelings, but I'm not George and I don't have anything like his patience."

"Would your leaving cause her any extra problems?"

"No. She's really quite self-sufficient, and a cleaning woman comes once a week to help with the work."

"Then, why the hesitation? Are you afraid of hurting her?"

"I don't know. I don't think so. She's always been closer to George, and she would probably enjoy having just him around. But I can hear her objections now. 'Go back to that town as a private tutor! What will your old friends think, and what about all the people we know?' Mother is always very concerned about what others think."

"Leave that part of it to me. You won't be coming to Quimper as a teacher but as a friend, to help me out. The children really need someone like you around!"

Pierre felt strange as he spoke, almost unable to recognize his own voice—a warm voice made more vibrant by his efforts to convince. Accustomed to controlling his emotions and usually able to choose his words carefully, he now was finding it difficult to contain his enthusiasm. Instead of calmly considering his decision, he could hardly think straight. For perhaps the first time in his life, he was acting on impulse.

Still unconvinced, Françoise continued to look at him, the green of her eyes even more intense in the sunlight. Pierre did not remember her being so beautiful. On the other hand, he had never before been so close to her. Actually, this was the first time he had been aware of her as a person . . . and a woman.

He was struck by a thought that brought lines of worry to his face.

"Françoise, there's something else I would like to ask you . . . even though it may seem to be none of my business. . . ."

He hesitated for a moment; it was a rather delicate subject.

"You told me you would like to return to Brittany, but, maybe—aside from your mother and brother—there's someone else who would like you to stay in Paris?"

"Someone else?"

"I mean, at your age, it wouldn't be surprising if you were engaged . . . or at least, well, you know. . . ."

He felt awkward, uncomfortable. This was a position he was not familiar with. Françoise was laughing.

"No. Not even a glimmer of hope from among my brother's friends. I must say they're not very romantic though. They're pure scientists."

"Thank God for science! What else could stand in your way—your students?"

"I have only two at present, and I only give them lessons in Latin. I'm sure they could find another tutor without any trouble."

"Well then, fair is fair! I'm offering you two in exchange. They're intelligent, charming and obedient, uhh, most of the time."

She smiled once more but did not answer. Her eyes wandered across the golden haze above the river. Pierre didn't want to interrupt her train of thought; he knew that Françoise was trying to consider the situation from all sides. The furthest thing from her mind when she had awakened that morning, the whole thing must be quite incredible to her; he didn't have to wait long to have his suspicions confirmed.

"There's a question I would like to ask you, too," she

said. "I remember your aunt very well. How do you think she'd react to having me in the house?"

Pierre felt as though someone had just stuck a knife into his stomach. His enthusiasm dropped considerably. This was one more thing to add to all the other incredible events of the day. Since meeting Françoise, he had completely forgotten about his aunt.

"Well, I have to admit that it could be a serious problem," he said.

"She's pretty bossy, isn't she?"

"To say the least! But just the same, she's still the nicest woman in the world; you only have to know how to handle her. I'm sure you two would get along just fine.

But his voice held little conviction, and it was largely to convince himself that he continued.

"You know, of course, that she had the highest regard for your father, for your whole family. Just last week, she was talking about you with great affection. If she's ever going to accept anyone looking after the children, surely it would be you!"

Once again, Pierre was surprised by his own assurance. All the favorable arguments came easily to mind, as though a little voice were telling him exactly what to say. He had only to listen to the voice and everything became quite simple.

"Veronique and Michel cannot be kept indefinitely under her strict thumb. They would be better off in a boarding school. Then at least they'd be with children their own age. But I really would rather find some other solution."

"Of course, you know you're blackmailing me!" she said reproachfully. "That's not fair! If you ever sent your children to a boarding school, I'd feel as though it was all my fault."

"Don't worry, it'll never happen. I know that for a

fact! I can see it in your eyes. You'll come to Quimper and they'll be very happy to have an older 'sister' to teach them and understand them. By the way, do you know how to drive?"

"I've had my license for a year. Why?"

"I'll give you one of the small company cars. After school, you can pick up the children and take them to the beach, so Aunt Elise can work as much as she wants around the house—which is what she'd rather do anyway! That way, everyone will be happy."

Pierre's enthusiasm was contagious. He could see his ideas making headway with Françoise as hope drove the doubt from her eyes. Her expression was like a child's, wonder-struck, yet timid, at the sight of a desired toy that had suddenly come within reach.

The obvious enchantment in Françoise's expression made Pierre wonder if perhaps he might be doing her a disservice. He was painting a very pretty picture, but the real situation might not be quite so easy to cope with. Was he setting her up for a rude awakening?

He continued to talk, but his tone of voice changed.

"I should caution you that my offer may be a little exaggerated. I have to admit that I really have no idea how my aunt will react, and I don't want you to have to live in an unpleasant environment. A number of things will have to be ironed out. But first, I must know if you're willing to come to Quimper. Would you be happy there?"

She raised her shoulders and her smile said it all.

"Answer me yes or no," he persisted.

"Yes, Pierre, I would be happy in Quimper."

"Thank you. And I would be happy to have you there! And that goes for the Sea Gull, too. But, two people who may not be delighted are your mother and my aunt. So, I think a great deal depends on the way we bring up the subject. It might not be a good idea to tell them the whole truth—"

"I hope you don't make suggestions like that in front of your children!"

"I don't mean we have to tell them out-and-out lies. Listen now, here's what I think we should say. We met accidentally—nothing too unusual about that, for I often come to Paris on business. We had lunch together and you told me how much you really missed Brittany. So naturally, I invited you to spend the Easter holidays in Quimper, as our guest. Once there, it'll be easy for you to stay."

"I'll feel like a phony and your aunt certainly won't like it."

"Wait a minute! One night, coming home from the office, I'll realize that since you've been there, the children's behavior has improved, my aunt looks better, and peace and happiness seemed to have come to the house. And then I'll say, as though it just occurred to me, that there's no rush for you to go back to Paris. I'll start to think that maybe . . . and so on. . . . "

"I'd never have believed you could be so conniving!"

"At my suggestion, the children will clap their hands, jump up, throw their arms around my neck and beg me to make you stay."

"And Aunt Elise will stalk out of the room, slamming the door behind her!"

"That's possible. But, if it doesn't work, I'll just have to think of something else. It's also possible that you'll find my children quite unbearable. Maybe you won't even want to stay. . . . "

Françoise made a gesture that implied the absurdity of such a possibility.

"But you have to think about it, Françoise! We can't decide anything in advance. All we can do is act like old friends. The Easter holidays will give us a chance to try things out. If the situation doesn't agree with you, you'll tell me, okay?"

"I promise. Anyway, I have a hard time hiding my feelings. If something is going wrong, you won't be able to miss it!"

"Every night, I'll check your eyes as if they were a pair of beautiful barometers."

"Don't forget to check your aunt's face, too!"

Delighted with their plan, they both laughed. Then Pierre looked at his watch.

"We found each other again exactly three hours and twenty-four minutes ago. I'm very happy about what's happened. In that short time, we've wiped out four years of separation and made plans that may solve serious problems for both of us—at least theoretically. All we have to do now is work out a few details. The Easter break is only a few days away, so we have to act quickly. To save time maybe we should go to see your mother right away. I could explain it to her myself—"

"I don't think that would be a good idea," interrupted Françoise. "When I called her a little while ago, I didn't mention my meeting you. I told her I was having lunch with a girlfriend. If she saw you, she'd be very suspicious. She'd wonder why you decided to invite me to your home, right out of the blue. . . ."

"With Aunt Elise for a chaperone? That should put her mind at ease."

"I think it would be better if I laid a little groundwork first. As soon as you get back to Quimper, write me a letter."

"The best way would be to have my Aunt Elise invite you. Don't laugh, now. It's not altogether impossible, you know. She'd certainly be happy to see you again and have you as her guest."

"For a few days, maybe, and only if I didn't usurp any of her authority!"

Her happy tone assured him that she was not too worried about it. Pierre matched her mood.

"I'm happy to see you're not underestimating the difficulties ahead! And that you seem to be able to take them with a smile!"

"No matter what we do, there are always problems."

Pierre looked at her with great emotion in his eyes.

"I'll be back home tonight. I have a plane reservation for ten to nine. I'll get a letter off to you tomorrow morning. Please say you'll come right away!"

"As soon as I can, I promise. I'll keep in touch by phone."

"Naturally, you understand that I will take care of expenses— No, I won't listen to any objections. We have to talk money sooner or later, and you mustn't be embarrassed about it. I'm a businessman and quite used to dealing with the subject. The best way is the direct way, so things don't lose their perspective. Let me worry about it. Don't concern yourself with finances."

He thought a moment before going on.

"I think we've covered everything. Is there anything else on the agenda? No? All right then, the meeting is adjourned. I suggest that the members of the board take another walk along the river. . . . "

He added, pointing at the river, "Our ship has hardly moved, yet we are almost in Quimper. The only thing missing are the sea gulls to welcome us home!"

They walked and talked, not noticing how quickly time passed. Françoise had a lesson to give, and at last they parted.

Pierre had some difficulty shaking her hand, as his arms were full of parcels: a truck for Michel, books for Veronique and a night-light for Aunt Elise.

"This is a peace offering," he had said, waiting in the boutique for the lamp to be wrapped. "To calm the wrath of the mighty keeper of my house!"

He had not been this happy for many years. He felt like a new man, and it had all happened in a few hours.

But when it came time to leave Françoise, something was troubling him. He did not feel like joking any more; he didn't have anything to say. No words could have expressed what he was feeling. He stood very still and looked deep into her eyes.

"See you soon?"

Pierre watched her as she disappeared through the entrance of her apartment building. As he stood there, he realized that in just a few hours, he had forgotten what loneliness was.

He headed for a taxi and was soon riding to Orly Airport. He was two and a half hours early! Waiting for departure time, he thought about Françoise. Even though he was leaving her behind, the feeling that he was very close to her stayed with him.

Handing the flight attendant his boarding pass, he noticed one more touch of the extraordinary to add to the delight of that memorable day. On the nose of the plane that would fly him home had been painted the name: "The Sea Gull."

Chapter 9

"I hope I'm not disturbing you?"

Farges was very surprised to see Perrelet coming into his office at three o'clock in the afternoon. It was totally inconsistent with the relationship that had been established between the two men over the years. It had been a long time since Perrelet had visited Farges.

"Please sit down. Is something wrong?"

"Not really. But I'd like to continue the conversation we started the other night. Monday, wasn't it? We were talking about a suitable person who could be groomed to replace me in the future."

"That again? I thought the matter was closed. I've told you what I think about it."

"Today, I would like you to hear my point of view. I've been thinking about it and I believe I've come up with the answer."

"Answer? What's the question? You told me that you weren't even considering retirement."

Perrelet gestured vaguely. "I certainly hope we're not going to wait for your son to take my place."

"Are you saying that he will never be able to?"

Farges had the harassed look of a man having a bad day. Perrelet ignored the question and sat down in a chair facing Farges.

"Research," he said, "is like fishing with a line. One must have the patience to sit for many hours in the heat or the cold, casting the line a hundred times, losing any number of hooks. . . . Your son does not lack intelligence, but I'm afraid he just wasn't cut out to be a fisherman."

Perrelet was smiling comfortably. Farges eyed the man through half-closed lids, toying nervously with his letter opener.

"So?" he asked dryly.

"But even if he was, it will be at least five years before he graduates. I don't know if it's my age or just exhaustion, but for some time now, I don't seem to have made any progress. I'm constantly improving my methods, but more and more often, I'm drawing blanks. Take that lotion I've been working on for the past year. You know that its effectiveness comes from the thallium salt, which is one of its components. Unfortunately, it's a toxic element and I don't seem to be able to neutralize it."

"In science, just like in any other discipline, not everything is necessarily possible."

"I'm positive there's a way. And I'm just as positive I'll never find it."

"All you need is a change of atmosphere. Take a week's holiday! Go south for a while; it'll do you good."

"No, it's more than that. I'm like an old fisherman who has lost his enthusiasm. I need someone to stimulate me, to carry me further. Someone young, if possible, who can throw his line more often and to a more distant point than I can throw mine. Then, maybe, with his help . . . ."

"All right. What do you suggest? Or, more precisely, whom do you have in mind?"

"I haven't forgotten what you said. If we were to hire a stranger, we'd risk seeing our manufacturing processes go to a competitor within six months. We need someone reliable, someone willing to become involved, who would have some sentimental ties with the business. Do you agree so far?"

Farges did not answer, did not make any sign; the letter opener was now quite still in his hands. Perrelet continued.

"It occurred to me that we'd never find anyone better than George Lachenaire."

"What?"

Farges almost jumped out of his chair. He looked at the chemist as if the man had completely lost his mind.

"Is this your idea of a joke?"

Perrelet sat very quietly, his gaze fixed on Farges, his blue eyes reflecting only surprise and innocence.

"You have some objection?"

"That's the understatement of the year! I was expecting anything but that! Listen, Perrelet, there's no use trying to discuss this any further. You have work to do and so have I. We're just wasting time."

With that, Farges stood up to signify that the interview was over. Astonished, Perrelet stayed in his seat.

"I must say, I don't understand your reaction. That boy has all the right qualifications: he has the education and the competence, and from what I understand, he's quite brilliant."

"How do you know? Have you kept in contact with the Lachenaire family?"

"No, I haven't. I don't like writing letters. But I have

gathered some information; I believe he intends to go into research and will be available in a few months."

"Fine. Then he'll surely have no trouble finding an interesting position. Is that all you came to see me about?"

"You have to admit that we certainly could trust the young man. The business was started by his father; he would consider it his own, and—"

"That is precisely why I don't want him here! No matter what! Believe me, I have good reason, but it's too complicated to explain."

Farges's voice had become calmer. One could almost see a smile on his face. He seemed to realize that the chemist, in his ignorance, had been well intentioned, and any further reaction from him might lead to questions he was not prepared to answer. He walked around his desk and put his hand on Perrelet's shoulder.

"No matter what happens, I thank you for your concern for the business. At first, your suggestion offended me, but now that I think about it I can see how you would think you had found a perfect solution to our problem."

"Are you saying that it does have merit?"

"Don't give the matter another thought. As far as my son is concerned, I expect you're right. If he doesn't get his degree in June, I'll send him on the road with the other salesmen so he can learn from them. And since you insist, I will seriously begin looking for someone to work with you."

As though discouraged, Perrelet shook his head.

"I'm sorry my idea doesn't appeal to you. I think George Lachenaire would be an excellent candidate. And as far as he's concerned, I'm sure he would like to work here."

"And take orders from me? I doubt it. In any case, I'll say it again: it's out of the question!"

"I'm sorry," repeated Perrelet. "Everyone would have seen it as a very nice gesture on your part," added Perrelet as he stood up. "People would have said 'how wonderful of Monsieur Farges to place George at the head of his father's lab.' "

Farges, who had gone back behind his desk, wheeled to face the chemist.

"It is no longer his father's laboratory," he shouted. "It's mine! And as to what people may say or think, I couldn't care less! Do you hear what I'm saying? I couldn't care less!"

"Well, I care."

"Really? And what business is it of yours?"

Perrelet ran his fingers through his white hair several times. He appeared very embarrassed.

"I have to agree it was none of my business until now," he confessed. "I wasn't even paying any attention. . . . "

"Paying attention to what? You're not getting through to me. What are you driving at?"

"Just rumors. You know how it is in a small town. Someone makes it big and everyone is jealous and the stories start going around. . . . "

"What stories? Are you talking about Madame Lachenaire and her complaints? All of that was forgotten a long time ago!"

"I'm afraid not. On the contrary, I have just received proof that it is very much remembered."

"What do you mean?"

"Well, I. . . . It's rather difficult to explain. Someone is angry with me for having done nothing to help the Lachenaire family . . . and . . . for having cooperated with you."

"Who is this someone?"

"I don't know. Whoever it is signs himself, 'The Sea Gull'!"

"Are you talking about a letter? An anonymous letter? Would you be talking about the letter you received Monday, the one that seemed to come from nowhere into your lab?"

Perrelet nodded.

"When you opened it, I thought I saw a picture of a bird!"

"A sea gull, yes."

"A sea gull that, according to you, was no more than an April Fools' Day joke! I suspected there was more to it than that. You seemed to be quite upset. But then, you told me it was just a joke. . . ."

"That's what I thought at first: a joke in very bad taste. Anyway, I couldn't say anything else at the time. I had to think about it."

"And after you had had time to think about it, you came to see me about hiring George Lachenaire!"

"That's about it. . . ."

Perrelet was becoming extremely embarrassed, and he lowered his head like a guilty child. Farges, on the other hand, had regained full control of himself, his face stern, his words clear and cold.

"Put yourself in my shoes," continued the chemist. "I have reached an age when I want a little peace and quiet. I don't want to get involved in anything. Maybe I'm wrong, taking this letter so seriously, but—"

"Show it to me!"

Startled, Perrelet raised his head and looked at his boss.

"I can't do that!"

"Why? Does it say something unpleasant about me?" Farges laughed uneasily. "Don't worry about it. Actually I'm beginning to find it all quite amusing. Where's the letter? Do you have it with you?"

"Please! Forget the letter."

"How can I? You've told me too much or too little. If you didn't want me to read it, you shouldn't have brought up the subject!"

As the chemist hesitated, Farges walked back to him. When he spoke he sounded almost jovial.

"I know you, Perrelet. You are too sensitive; you worry too much. Since last Monday, you probably haven't slept well. You want to be at peace with everyone, even those you don't know. This business about George Lachenaire is proof of that. A suggestion of this . . . Sea Gull, right?"

Sighing, the chemist pulled the letter from his pocket.

"After all . . . you might as well know about it. But, I hope you won't be angry at me. . . . "

Farges shrugged. Perrelet handed over the letter and watched Farges's reaction: he turned white and his mouth fell open.

"A swindler, would you believe," he muttered as he read. "Well, thank God, at least I'm not being accused of killing Lachenaire!"

At last he returned the letter to Perrelet.

"This is garbage! The whole thing is preposterous! Whoever wrote this must be out of his mind. I'm surprised that a man of your caliber would fall for something like this."

"Well, I can't help wondering. . . . Remember how the letter got there? I asked the caretaker; he told me that he hadn't brought it up and I believe him." He paused a moment. "So it must be someone who works here."

"Maybe. It shouldn't be too difficult to find out who it was. I already have some ideas."

Perrelet looked at Farges in surprise.

"You mean you know who wrote the letter?"

"Not exactly, no; but I know if I think about it for a while . . . . We'll talk about it later. For the time being, forget the whole thing, and for God's sake stop worrying, even if I never hire George Lachenaire!

"You have done what was asked of you," added Farges as he led the chemist to the door. "From here on in, this affair is between me and the Sea Gull!"

Chapter 10

For the third time in the space of an hour, Pierre appeared at the door of Mme Rogues's office. She had never seen him in such a state; and even more extraordinary, he didn't even appear to realize that he was behaving strangely.

"I think my watch must have stopped. Is it really only three-thirty?"

"Not quite, monsieur. I didn't hear the convent bell chime the half hour yet."

"Good! I'll still have time to dictate a few letters before going to the train station. You did say the train came in at four twenty-three? Come to think of it, I've already given you enough letters to do today. Maybe I'd better go over to the contractor's and see how the plans for the new plant are coming along."

"I called him yesterday, monsieur. There will be nothing new before next week."

"That's right, you told me that this morning. Sorry, I

forgot. It's probably just as well. That man talks so much, I'd likely get stuck and miss meeting the train."

Seeing the surprised look on his secretary's face, he felt that he had to explain.

"It wouldn't be very polite to leave Mademoiselle Lachenaire waiting. My aunt would be very upset—she's the one who invited her."

Mme Rogues, putting a new ribbon on her typewriter, appeared quite casual as she asked, "Your aunt invited her?"

"Well, she . . . I . . . well, yes and no. I told you how I met Mademoiselle Lachenaire by accident while I was in Paris. She was dying to come and spend some time in Quimper and I told her that possibly, perhaps . . . during the Easter holidays. . . . I was thinking of the children, of course . . . two weeks with my aunt . . . you know what I mean. She impressed me very much, and I'm sure she'll be very good for the children."

Mme Rogues wondered where the aunt's invitation came in, but she did not voice her thoughts. She smiled to herself, but Pierre didn't appear to notice.

"It certainly seems to be a good thing for everyone," she said approvingly. Then after a short silence, "Except, perhaps, for you!"

"Why do you say that?"

"Well, I'm sure you'll feel that you shouldn't leave that girl with your aunt all the time. At least in the beginning, you'll have to go out with her when she takes the children for walks. . . . "

She sounded so sincere that no one could ever have accused her of being otherwise.

"Do you think so?" asked Pierre, beaming.

"I know so. As head of the house, you'll have certain obligations and, knowing you and how much time you devote to the business . . . ."

Pierre sighed.

"I'll try. It's time I learned to forget about work once in a while."

He glanced again at his watch.

"Maybe I'd better leave now if I want to find a parking spot close to the station."

Mme Rogues figured that her boss would arrive at the station long before the arrival of the train. He certainly was very concerned about treating Mademoiselle Lachenaire with the utmost courtesy!

"Will you come back later today to sign the letters?"

"Of course. I'll be here by six at the latest."

"What if Monsieur Farges calls again?"

"Oh! I forgot to call him back. Tell him I'm very sorry . . . that I'm tied up. . . . "

After the door had closed behind him, Mme Rogues sat and daydreamed for a long while, smiling to herself in wry amusement at her employer's behavior.

Pierre wandered up and down the platform. The last thing his secretary had said stuck in his mind, and he felt badly about avoiding Farges. It had been two weeks since they had met. That had been the night he had dinner with Mireille. . . .

He had not seen her since and hadn't even talked to her on the phone, although he had called once. She had gone to spend some time in Switzerland with a cousin and had not tried to reach him. The Sea Gull's letter seemed to have put an end to their relationship.

It was over, Pierre told himself, and somehow, he felt no regret.

But on the other hand, he was embarrassed to meet Farges. He had received a large order from the man and should have taken him out for dinner, at least dropped in to see him. But Pierre had only called Farges once, and even then, the Sea Gull had made his presence felt; he couldn't ignore the accusations in his aunt's letter.

Farges must have been surprised at his attitude, because he was a good customer and a friend. Pierre wondered if Mireille had shown her father the letter she had received at the restaurant. Perhaps she had preferred to give him another explanation for the sudden break in their relationship.

Thinking about it, Pierre realized that "relationship" was too strong a word to describe what he and Mireille had shared. No commitments, no promises; they had really been little more than casual acquaintances. If the whole town considered them engaged, it was because Mme Farges had interpreted her own wishes as realities. It wasn't important any more. And Farges was too intelligent to mix sentiment with business. As far as Mireille was concerned, she would not take long to become involved with someone else.

The situation with Aunt Elise, however, was really giving Pierre something to worry about. When he had introduced the idea of a visit from Françoise, his aunt had been quite shocked.

"I find this invitation quite unbecoming," she had said. "And I'm surprised that a young woman as well brought up as Françoise would even consider it!"

"What are you trying to say?" Pierre had asked. "I really don't see why—"

"You seem to forget that we live in a small town; everyone will be talking."

"Well, I'm surprised that a woman as intelligent as you would pay any attention to what —"

"I have to. I'm thinking of your position, of the children. . . ."

Pierre had jumped at the opportunity.

"Precisely! The children will provide an excellent excuse."

"Excuse? So now you have to find excuses! It just goes to show that you feel guilty about it."

"But I don't, Aunt Elise! You're putting words in my

mouth. I'm just trying to understand your objections by discussing them with you. There are plenty of families, even here in Quimper, that hire young women to look after their children."

"Families, yes; not widowers living alone."

"But I'm not living alone; you're here! You practically run the house."

"It's not the same thing and you know it! Françoise will be putting herself in a compromising situation!"

"That kind of thinking belongs in another century! Anyway, she doesn't care."

"How do you know? Did she tell you?"

"We didn't even consider that aspect of it, let alone discuss it."

"That's what I thought; neither of you is showing any consideration. You're simply not thinking. She may be excused because she's young; probably she isn't aware of the full implications of this, but you at your age —"

"What am I supposed to be—a decrepit old man? In that case, there's nothing for you to worry about!"

The scene had taken place early on Wednesday, the morning after Pierre had returned from Paris. The children had left for school and Odile's vacuum cleaner had provided the background for the discussion. Aunt Elise was in her element; to her, this kind of argument was like food to a starving man.

"By the way, Pierre, what did you mean that her being here might be good for the children? Surely, you're not thinking about turning over the children's upbringing and education to Françoise?"

This was not the first time Pierre had noticed his aunt's keen intuitive powers. He had hesitated for a moment; why not bring everything out into the open and get it over with? He decided to stick to his original plan: wait and be patient. Françoise hadn't even been to the house yet, so why fight about something that was still so uncertain?

"I mentioned the children just to reassure you," he had said calmly. "Saying that Françoise is coming here on account of the children would stop all the gossip in town. It's up to you, how you want to look at it. As far as I'm concerned, I don't have to make excuses to anyone."

Seeing that his aunt was ready to explode, he had added, "Except to you, of course. But, knowing your love for the Lachenaire family, I was hoping you'd be pleased at the idea of inviting Françoise here."

"I'm not arguing; little Françoise was always quite charming, but —"

"And furthermore, knowing how much work you do in the house, I thought it would be a great help if she were to look after the children during the Easter holidays. It would certainly take some of the load off your shoulders. As a matter of fact, I even thought you might be glad to write and invite her yourself. . . . "

Pierre never would have believed that he could lie with such sincerity. He was going to play his little act to the end. Before finishing his last sentence, he had grabbed his coat, apparently very upset by his aunt's reaction.

"Once again, you have twisted my best intentions. That's all right; I'll call her this morning and tell her that I was wrong and that you don't want her in this house. She was looking forward to coming back to the Brittany she loves so much. It will be a very rude awakening for her, because she holds you in such high regard. Oh, well . . . I'd rather have it this way than have her walk in where she isn't welcome!"

At that, he had left, slamming the door. As he had expected, Aunt Elise was beside him by the time he reached the garage.

"It's not a question of her not being welcome! Nor is it a question of canceling the invitation, since you have already been thoughtless enough to invite her."

"Then, what do you suggest?"

"Well, you may call her if you wish, but only to tell her that everything's all right at this end. There's nothing else we can do. I'll write a little note to Madame Lachenaire—not to tell her that I'm overjoyed, believe me! Simply to tell her not to worry, that the invitation is from me and quite proper. . . . "

"I really don't see why you feel you have to do that, but let's not get into it again. . . . "

Pierre had lowered his head to hide his delight. Then, so Aunt Elise would not feel badly about losing the argument, he added, "Maybe Françoise will help us find out who this Sea Gull is. Did you hear anything more?"

"Nothing. I've been wondering if anyone else has received the same type of letter."

"Yes."

"Who?"

"A maniac rarely contents himself with just one disturbance," had been all he had answered.

Pierre was smiling to himself as he waited for the train. Poor Aunt Elise! What would have been her reaction if he had shown her his own letter? That day, when he left the house, he had felt as happy as a child who had finally wangled permission for something he had wanted to do for a long time. Without hearing a word Mme Rogues was saying about what had happened in his absence, Pierre had entered his office and called Paris.

Now a week had gone by since he had seen Françoise—a week that seemed like a year. Time had stood still the moment he'd heard Françoise's voice over the phone saying that her mother was quite agreeable to her spending some time in Quimper. She would arrive the following Thursday on the four twenty-three. . . . The clock in the railway station showed four twenty-one. The platform had come alive. Pulling himself out of his reverie, Pierre recognized several people and nodded politely.

Passing a doorway guarded by a security officer, he noticed Mme Farges in the waiting room and wondered why she was there. He didn't have to wait long for the answer.

The train was pulling into the station. The doors opened and people loaded with luggage began to fill the platform. Pierre strained his eyes, trying to find that one slim form among the crowd.

"Hello! I didn't expect to see you here!" The voice, right beside him, made him jump.

Sun-tanned and smiling, looking quite delighted to see him, was Mireille. Obviously, she misunderstood his reason for being there, thinking that Pierre had come to meet her in the hope of a reconciliation.

He felt acute embarrassment coupled with annoyance. His feelings were quite evident in his expression.

"You're just returning from the winter games?" he mumbled, his eyes scanning the platform over her shoulder. Mireille caught on right away and blushed, angry at herself for being so presumptuous.

"Forgive me," she said dryly. "It was very stupid of me to think . . . ." She proceeded to pick up her suitcase.

"I didn't know you were coming home today. I'm waiting for a friend of my aunt's. But I'm glad to run into you."

"Sure you are. It's written all over your face. See you. . . ."

"Listen, Mireille, I . . . at least, let me help you with your suitcase!"

"Please! Don't waste any of your precious time with me!"

As he watched her walk away, he felt badly, but also furious. Today, of all days, and on the same train . . . . He shook his head at the unlucky coincidence.

Three seconds later, Mireille no longer existed, had never existed. There was no one else on the platform— even the train had disappeared into thin air. All Pierre could see was a young face, younger than he remembered, just a few feet away.

"Françoise . . . I was beginning to worry!"

He had taken her hands, clasped them in his, fighting the desire to kiss her, fighting the burning feeling surging through him. Had they been anywhere else, he might have taken her into his arms.

She looked at him anxiously, noticing his distress and the longing in his eyes.

"You were talking to Mireille Farges," she remarked. "I would have come over to say hello, but I saw her this morning at the Montparnasse station and again on the train; both times she acted as though she didn't know me."

"She's a silly girl. But her father is my biggest customer. Here, let me take your suitcase."

Time had started to move again; life was picking up its rhythm once more. All the people and things that had momentarily disappeared were there again. And he was conscious that Françoise and he were being observed with a great deal of curiosity.

"Not everyone is like Mireille," he declared. "The decent people of Quimper are happy to see you. Tonight, you will probably be the main topic of conversation around the tables. People will talk about . . . oh . . . how the lost sheep has been found. I can see myself very well playing the role of the good shepherd!"

As they turned to leave the station, Mireille nudged

her mother and nodded in the couple's direction. Mme Farges eyes followed them as they strolled off together.

"Well, that explains a lot of things. I think we'll soon know who sent that nasty letter. Now I agree with you: the Sea Gull must be a woman!"

Chapter 11

Pierre took the long way home to give Françoise time to recapture her memories of Quimper, the town she had loved so much as a child. It was like turning the pages of an old scrapbook.

He had dropped his lighthearted tone, for seeing her again reawakened the same emotions he had felt when he'd left her the week before: a strange mixture of anguish and happiness. He found he was able to say only very mundane things to her.

"The trip didn't tire you too much? I would rather have had you come by plane!"

His voice was shaking a little, his throat was dry, and his heart was pounding. No one had ever before made him feel like this. He wanted so much to be tender, to tell her not to worry, that he would protect her. Even Regine had not stirred such feelings. Of course he had loved his wife very much, but they had been equals. She had been his companion, his friend, going hunting with him, spending hours in the bush when he wouldn't even worry about how she felt. Regine had been strong, as strong as his love for her.

Françoise was so much younger than he, so vulnerable. . . .

Taking advantage of a stoplight, he lit a cigarette and slowly blew the smoke in front of him, as if the action would relieve him of this unique feeling. Did she guess? Did she share his state of mind? Françoise was not saying a word.

"Happy?" he asked.

She turned to smile at him, but her eyes were unfathomable pools.

"I don't know . . . I realize it must sound stupid, but I really don't. Sometimes happiness is difficult to recognize."

"Funny, I was thinking the same thing. For the past few days, I've been trying to imagine the moment I would see you again, the moment you would be close to me, like this, in the car. . . . "

It was happening to him again; words were pouring out of his mouth before he could stop them. He had intended to say something ordinary, but had no sooner spoken than he realized he was using the language of love. Françoise stared straight ahead, as though concentrating on the gray streets ahead.

"Until now, everything was simple. I didn't even consider that you might not come. And now that you are here, I'm wondering if I've done the right thing, dragging you here."

The look she gave him was uneasy.

"I'm afraid I let myself get carried away in a moment of pure selfishness," he explained. "I was thinking more about my children and how much I wanted to see you again. Now, I'm thinking of you. I hope this won't prove to be a foolish move. And, Françoise, I truly hope you will be happy here."

"Did something happen since we talked to each other on the phone ? Your aunt . . . ?"

"My aunt seems to be looking forward to your coming. Mind you, there's no guarantee she won't be unpleasant."

"I think I can cope with her. The children?"

"They are anxiously waiting to meet you. No, Françoise, nothing new has happened . . . nothing . . . except in me."

"I see. You've had second thoughts, is that it? You've decided you don't want me here?"

She was doing her best to keep the conversation as light as possible. Pierre refused to go along.

"I've realized how important your happiness is to me. I would feel very badly if you were to regret coming here."

She rested her hand on his arm.

"There are always risks to be taken, unless you decide never to leave your own little world to explore someone else's, unless you refuse to live. . . . Stop worrying, Pierre. Coming out of the station, I didn't speak because memories were choking me. I can answer the question you asked me a little while ago: Yes, I am happy! And I will be happy in your home . . . I know I will be . . . no matter what. "

Pierre turned to look at her, hoping to see in her face confirmation that he had been right in interpreting what she had just said to be a declaration of love. But Françoise kept her eyes straight ahead.

"In any case," she continued, "don't forget that we are obeying the Sea Gull's orders. If anyone is to be held responsible for whatever might happen, it's him."

Aunt Elise was waiting for them in the hallway when they got home. Whatever else she may have been, she had to be admired for one quality: she did have a certain sense of ceremony. To greet Françoise, she had carefully dressed in her Sunday best. The welcome speech she made was not particularly original, but quite definitely correct.

"Welcome to this house, my dear child. I liked your father very much and I'm happy to see how much like him you are. Your mother was also a very good friend; I'm sorry she could not come with you. Come now, you must be tired. I'll show you to your room."

"Where are the children?" asked Pierre.

"They've been sent to their room until it's time for dinner. Veronique was half an hour late getting home from her piano lesson. She met one of her friends and, would you believe this, they spent their time wandering around the supermarket. As for Michel, well, he's been quite impossible! I gave him a piece of strawberry pie after lunch and he dropped it in the yard. You wouldn't believe the word he used! I heard him from the kitchen. And wouldn't you know, Mademoiselle Karadrec was walking by at that very moment. . . ."

For Françoise's benefit, she filled in a little background.

"Our neighbor, Mademoiselle Karadrec, has the most vicious tongue in the county! All of Quimper will know tomorrow that the Lalonde children use filthy language. . . . Is something funny?"

Pierre managed to contain the laugh that was tickling in his throat. This was not the time to argue.

"Not at all; I'll go up and have a word with those two myself. But I want them to meet Françoise. Couldn't we call a truce in her honor?"

"I knew it. Every time I punish the children, you do something to spoil them!"

"I don't want to start anything. I just thought—"

"In bringing up children, there's nothing worse than inconsistency. Well, I've said my piece. You're their father; do what you want!"

Pierre was furious and all set to argue. Françoise quickly stepped in.

"If you don't mind, I'd rather meet the children later. I'd like to freshen up after that long train ride."

Aunt Elise calmed down immediately.

"I don't blame you, my dear. There's no hurry. You'll have your hands full soon enough!" Turning to Pierre, she said, "Of course, you're going back to the office?"

That was all Pierre needed to decide to stay.

"No, I'm not going back to the office. I'll just call Madame Rogues and ask her to bring over the letters I have to sign."

"Normally—"

"Normally, Françoise is not here. I'm not about to leave her alone in this big house, with the children in their room and you in your kitchen!"

"Thank you for the lesson in etiquette! This way, Françoise."

A minute later, Françoise was in her room, trying to register all the information that Elise was delivering in a rapid-fire style any auctioneer would envy.

"Here is a dresser for your things—that drawer doesn't close very well. A closet for your dresses— watch out for the lock; I have it oiled the first Tuesday of every month. See this little porcelain vase? Pierre likes it very much; it used to be his mother's. . . . The washroom is at the end of the hallway, to your left— don't forget to turn off the hot water heater after your bath. If you need anything, just ask. But ask me, not Odile. She's a good woman, but she has a way of confusing everything. There, I'll leave you on your own. I must prepare dinner."

Her hand on the door handle, she hesitated and turned to look at Françoise.

"I'm afraid you may have a very bad first impression

of me. You mustn't think I'm always picking on Pierre. Usually, we get along on major issues and our little tiffs are never serious. He's a good boy and I'm very fond of him. There's only one thing about him that really annoys me: he wants to be right all the time!"

Françoise was finishing dressing when she heard footsteps in the hallway and children's voices. Opening the door, she saw two little figures disappear into the room next to hers. Smiling, she followed Veronique and Michel into the room. They were both sitting quietly at a table, apparently concentrating on a very difficult lesson.

"Hello!"

Not a peep. Veronique's head hardly moved. Michel lowered his head even deeper into the book. Françoise came closer and looked down at the book that the boy seemed to find so fascinating. It was upside down. She didn't mention it, but her smile widened.

"Don't you want to be friends?"

This time, a part of a nose, one eye and one rosy cheek became visible above the bent elbow.

"You won't tell on us?"

"Tell on you? About what?"

"Because we weren't supposed to leave our room," explained Veronique. "We are being punished."

"I know, your Aunt Elise told me, but that's none of my business."

Both children had left their chairs and were examining Françoise very closely. They looked very serious.

"We already saw you. We were at the window when you arrived."

"Do I get a hug?"

Michel was the first to jump up and put his arms around Françoise's neck.

"You smell nice," he said delightedly.

Veronique moved a little closer, but seemed much

more reserved. When she spoke, her voice sounded very grown up.

"You should be more polite, Michel. You don't just jump on somebody like that!"

"Why not? Papa told us that Françoise was coming here to play with us!"

"That doesn't give you the right to jump all over her. You'll see what Aunt Elise will have to say if she hears about it!"

"She'll have no reason to be upset," interrupted Françoise. "Michel is right. And I need a hug from you, too. Otherwise, I'll think you don't want to be my friend, and that would hurt me very much. I hope you don't think I'm too old?"

"Oh, no! There's not that much difference between you and me; I know you're twenty-three, and that means that you're not old enough to be my mother!"

"Then I can be your older sister. Is that all right with you?"

"Oh, yes! But if I do something wrong, will you tell Aunt Elise?"

"The best way would be not to do anything wrong!"

"I know. But sometimes, I can't help it."

"I'll never tell on you."

"Are you afraid of her, too?"

"A little; but I don't want her to know."

All three were quiet for a moment as they enjoyed their little conspiracy. And at that moment, Françoise seemed as young and innocent as her two new friends.

She walked over to Veronique's desk and saw that she had been studying a history book.

"I thought you were on holidays as of this morning?" she asked in surprise.

"Aunt Elise wants us to do some work every day. I was trying to learn tomorrow's lesson. It's about some old kings and it's boring. Are you going to be working with us?"

"Maybe. But, I think we should have some fun together, too. Better still, let's try to do both at the same time; we'll have fun while we're working."

Michel laughed heartily. "We'll never be able to do that!"

"Of course we will! We'll go to the beach or the country every day. We'll collect shells and put them into boxes; maybe pick some plants and flowers and paste them in a book. We'll watch the insects and see how they live."

"What are insects? Are they bad?"

Veronique threw up her hands in disbelief.

"It all depends," answered Françoise. "There are some that sting, like mosquitoes and bees. Insects are all the animals that fly except birds."

"Airplanes?"

Michel looked warily at his sister out of the corner of his eye. But this time, Veronique didn't rise to the bait. Instead she asked, "Will we have to follow a schedule?"

"What do you mean?"

"Well, now we get up at eight, have breakfast, wash and get dressed. Then we can play until ten o'clock. From ten to eleven, we have to do some homework. After lunch, we rest until three o'clock; I guess that's the worst part. After that—"

"No," said Françoise, knowing she was treading on dangerous ground. "Let's not follow a schedule. We are on holidays, after all! But we'll have to try to be here on time for meals!"

Michel jumped with joy, clapping his hands.

"You're super!" he cried. Then he brought up what obviously would be the main stumbling block. "Aunt Elise will have a fit!" He was looking at Françoise with something akin to worship.

"But we mustn't upset too many things; we wouldn't want to hurt your aunt's feelings. I'll do my best to make her understand that we can learn just as much by walking in the woods as by burying our heads in books. Now, let's take a look at that history lesson, Veronique!"

And very soon, with the enraptured children sitting on either side of her on the sofa, Françoise brought history to life: caravans pulled by oxen following roads scarcely visible across prairies and through forests; a huge man being carried high on the shoulders of soldiers with iron leggings, with more soldiers on horseback surrounding him.

"Why didn't he do anything, if he was the king?" asked Michel. "That's not right!"

"Oh, why don't you be quiet and let Françoise talk!"

"I would have liked being a soldier or horseback."

Veronique just looked at Françoise and smiled.

"I think I'll remember this lesson very well. It's funny; you're saying the same thing as the book, but it sounds so different."

Michel had his own explanation.

"That's because Françoise is beautiful."

Someone laughed in the doorway. It was Pierre. Michel's comment allowed him to take a light tone, and at the same time, gave him a chance to relieve his tension.

"My son seems to have very good taste," he said, "and also shows signs of being a psychologist!"

Françoise was blushing.

"You mustn't say things like that, Michel."

"Why can't I, when it's true? You are beautiful and you smell nice. Is it okay if I hug you again?"

"I have the feeling that our troubles with that one are over," said Pierre.

"I like Françoise," declared Michel. "We aren't going

to have a nap after lunch anymore and we're going to play with bees and Aunt Elise isn't going to have anything to say about it! There!"

Françoise gently put her hand on the boy's head.

"That's not quite the way it may happen," she corrected him. "I may have taken on more than it will be possible for me to do. We all have to do our best to try and have fun and please Aunt Elise at the same time."

"Papa, why didn't Françoise come here sooner?"

"I've just been asking myself the same question," murmured Pierre, not looking at Françoise.

THAT EVENING, Françoise, Pierre and Elise were relaxing in the living room.

Elise, sitting in an Empire sofa, appeared to be knitting in a competition. The needles danced in her fingers with mechanical precision and perfect timing.

"I have never seen anyone knit so fast and so well at the same time!" Françoise couldn't help remarking.

Elise's needlework was indeed something to behold. Very much aware of the young woman's admiration, Elise kept going as though she was trying to beat her own record.

The children were sleeping and Odile, who lived close by, had left for the night. The living room was lit by a single lamp, which made the room seem larger and yet more intimate. Logs burned quietly in the fireplace, the flames creating a fantastic spectacle of light and shadow in the room.

Sitting just outside the halo of light, Pierre was quietly smoking, rediscovering sensations he had long forgotten. He was very happy just to be there enjoying the peace and quiet of the evening, his mind empty of thought.

There hadn't been an evening like this since Regine's death. Usually, when he had dinner at home, he would leave the dining room and go straight to his study to look over some projects and production reports. To him the house was just an extension of his office. Aunt Elise, who liked to read in bed, would not stay downstairs alone too long.

But tonight had all the makings of a pleasant evening: the lamp, the fire, the smell of wood, and outside, a light rain.

The first evening with Françoise . . . Pierre could hardly believe it. It seemed that the picture of this young woman—the fine lines of her body, the slight movement of her hair where light from the fire played softly—had always been in his mind. Perhaps, it was because he had dreamed so much about it in the past few days; or was it the answer to a secret desire he was realizing only now, one that had been very much a part of him for some time?

Françoise watched him with the same kind of anxiety in her eyes as she had shown at the train station, just a few hours earlier. He sensed her unspoken questions: "Why aren't you saying anything? Are you unhappy? Displeased? Is my presence here bringing back sad memories?"

If Elise had not been there, Françoise might have asked these questions aloud. Pierre would then have come closer to her, taken her face in his hands and reassured her, shown her the happiness in his eyes. Or he would have walked over and sat on the floor in front of her, resting against her knees like a child.

These thoughts, this life in their eyes when they looked at each other, this tenderness, so sweet, yet somehow painful—surely these resembled the signs of love. Pierre was very much aware of it. He felt it the first moment he had seen her again in the church.

A part of him that he had thought buried had come alive. He was able to love, to hope once more. . . . He was young again . . . like an injured man finally recovering the use of his muscles. . . .

The thought of Mireille, however, forced him to be cautious. Two weeks earlier, he had thought perhaps he loved her, and had it not been for the Sea Gull's intervention, he might have married her. One line kept returning to his mind: "She would never consider your children as her own. . . . "

He recalled the scene in the children's room before dinner. Then, after the meal, the way Françoise, without seeming to notice Aunt Elise's disapproving look, led the children to bed, tucking them in and kissing them good night. . . .

The persistent ring of the front door bell pulled Pierre from his reverie. Elise almost jumped out of her seat.

"Who could that possibly be at this time of night . . . ?"

The clock on the mantel showed nine-thirty.

"Maybe Odile forgot something!"

"She has a key. Why would she ring the bell?"

Pierre stood up and walked to the door.

"You'd think people would stay home on a night like this!"

Surprised and a little concerned, he threw a raincoat over his shoulders and ran across the yard to the gate. He could see no one through the ironwork.

No one in the dimly lit street either, as he opened the gate and peered up and down the road. There were a few parked cars but no sound of a running motor; only the patter of rain striking the cobblestones reached his ears.

Annoyed, Pierre closed the gate with a bang. What idiot could have played that kind of joke?

Unconsciously, he glanced at the mailbox and noticed a letter in the slot. It was addressed to him and marked "Personal." The word was underlined twice.

Back in the hallway, he opened it quickly. A glance was all he needed. There were only three words in the middle of the sheet: "Very well done!"

It was signed, "The Sea Gull."

Chapter 12

At the sound of an approaching car Pierre got up to look out his office window. The red Mercedes Michel and his friends called the "fire chief's car" had pulled into the parking lot. Almost immediately, his intercom buzzed. The woman at the reception desk was calling.

"Monsieur Farges has arrived, monsieur. Shall I direct him to your office?"

"No, I'll come down."

It was the least he could do. Rushing down the stairs, Pierre was not feeling too pleased with himself, well aware he had treated his best customer rather badly. Farges must have thought so, too, because he had had his secretary call Pierre's secretary to make an appointment. Under ordinary circumstances, he would have called Pierre himself. Mme Rogues had seemed quite surprised at the message she had given to Pierre.

"Monsieur Farges would like to know if you can see him in about an hour. . . ."

The unexpected call made Pierre uneasy. Perhaps it meant that the business dealings between Farges and himself wouldn't be going too well. When they met, however, his words were cordial: "Dear friend. . . ." "So much work. . . . " "Sorry about this. . . . " And so on. Farges had not made any objection, but he seemed rather distant. When they reached Pierre's office, he even refused the traditional whisky. And Pierre had had the bar installed especially for Farges.

"I was just wondering if you were sick, or if perhaps you were having production problems with your new packaging?"

Farges was wasting no time—immediate reference to the latest order, followed by a veiled threat, all in one breath.

"If that's the case, my dear fellow, you mustn't hesitate to tell me about it. We'll try to work out another solution together. . . ." That could only mean another supplier. . . .

Pierre decided to put his cards on the table and set things straight. What he had to say had very little to do with business.

"Let me at least offer you an explanation—No, no! I quite understand! I know very well that my attitude must seem somewhat strange, if not downright offensive."

"Well, my wife and I were worried; we thought perhaps we might have offended you without realizing it."

"And you thought I was sulking like a small child? No, I was simply embarrassed because of . . . my relationship with Mireille."

"You had an argument? Sometimes that's good! You know, adds spice to the affair. And not only that, making up can be a lot of fun!"

"Well, in the first place, we didn't have a fight. And I think I should tell you, as well, that Mireille and I are not in love with each other."

For a moment Farges sat quite still and looked at Pierre. When he finally spoke, his voice was very controlled.

"You mean to say you discovered that, just like that —" he snapped his fingers "—one day?"

"Let's just say that we both realized it at about the same time. At least, that's what I think; I haven't really discussed it with Mireille. We haven't seen each other since the night we had dinner on—" he looked at the calendar on the desk "—the twenty-eighth of March. Of course, aside from last Thursday when we ran into one another at the station."

"You were waiting for someone, I understand."

"I called Mireille, but she wasn't home. If she had wanted to see me, surely she would have returned my call."

"And if you had wanted to see her, you would have kept calling!"

Pierre merely shrugged in a gesture of resignation.

"I sincerely believe that we were not meant for each other."

Farges got up from his chair and walked over to the window to gaze out into the distance.

"That's too bad," he sighed. "For once, my wife and I agreed on something; the idea of a marriage between you two pleased us very much. We didn't want our daughter to marry one of those fools who are constantly vying for her attention. You are a solid and serious man; I was delighted at the idea of having a friend for a son-in-law—a friend and an associate, because our two businesses, by the same token, would have made an excellent marriage."

"Yes. I'm sorry, too. Mireille is a beautiful girl and I find her very attractive. Perhaps too attractive."

"You'd rather marry someone you don't find attractive?"

"Please try to understand. I'm not a teenager. At my

age, a great deal of consideration must be given to such matters. I have learned to control myself, especially in a situation as important as this one. What I am trying to say is that my attraction to Mireille was largely physical. And I don't think she was all that attracted to me."

"That's what a man always says when he leaves a woman—it gets rid of the guilt feelings. In any case, passion cools very quickly—a great love affair or a marriage of convenience, there's little difference. The end result is usually the same."

"I'm afraid I can't agree with you."

"That only proves that you aren't as old as you think you are; you still have a few illusions. On the other hand, I think that you are easily influenced."

"Why do you say that?"

Farges did not answer right away. One corner of his mouth turned up in a wry smile, and he began to pace the room. He stopped in front of Pierre's desk.

"Mireille showed me her letter from the Sea Gull."

Pierre was not particularly surprised; it was quite natural, under the circumstances, that the girl would want her parents' opinion on the matter. At any rate, he was totally indifferent. This meeting was beginning to bore him; he was anxious to see Farges leave. Besides, he had told Françoise and the children that he would meet them at the beach, some fifteen miles up the coast. It was getting late and he had promised to be there by five. He glanced at his watch and was relieved to see that he still had plenty of time.

"I would hate to think that the letter had anything to do with your sudden change of attitude toward Mireille," continued Farges, "yet . . . . "

"Let's just say it made both of us aware that we had little in common and made us realize quite clearly what a blunder we were about to make!"

"Then you agree with the Sea Gull?"

"I don't necessarily approve of the way he goes about things, but I have to give him credit, even while I'm wondering why he's so interested in us!"

"You mean you don't know?"

"I don't have a clue."

Farges had started pacing again. *You'd think he was in his own office*, thought Pierre, beginning to become annoyed. Aloud, he said, "Really, I haven't the slightest idea! Since that letter—that is to say for three weeks now—I've been trying to figure out what the point is to all this, but I haven't been able to make head nor tail of it."

Farges started to laugh.

"But, it's so simple! I'm surprised that a man like you, intelligent, reasonable, used to thinking things out . . . . True, you probably don't have all the pieces of the puzzle. You don't know, for instance, that Mireille was not the only one to receive a letter from the Sea Gull. . . ."

Pierre could not hide his surprise; immediately, he thought about his aunt. No, she would never have talked to Farges without telling him first, Pierre decided.

"You know Perrelet, my chemist? He received a letter, too—I won't go into details—and do you know what the Sea Gull asked him to do in that letter? To make a long story short, he wants George Lachenaire to come and work in my lab!"

"I really don't see what that has to do with Mireille."

"I didn't see any connection either, until the day that . . . ."

Frowning, Pierre observed Farges with some concern. The strange smile on the man's face did nothing to mellow his harsh expression. Farges took out a cigarette, tapped it on the desk a few times and brought it to his lips. Then, in dry tones, he finished, "until the day I learned that Françoise Lachenaire was back here." Pierre was startled.

"What's that have to do with anything? Surely, you don't think that . . . ?"

"I'm just trying to put the pieces together. Doesn't it seem strange to you? On the one hand, George, on the other, Françoise . . . . Everything seems to point to the fact that the Lachenaire family wants to come back to live in Quimper!"

"What are you driving at? Françoise is here only because my aunt invited her!"

"Oh, really? Do you expect me to believe that your aunt would be capable of such a friendly gesture?"

"How dare you!"

Pierre stood up, as if to put himself at a better advantage while confronting the enemy. He accepted it now: before him stood the enemy. Farges's face was filled with hatred. He was a threatened man who had decided to throw the first punch.

"Are you sure your aunt didn't receive an anonymous letter, too ?" he asked. "Couldn't she have been following the Sea Gull's instructions, when she invited Françoise? It's just too much of a coincidence otherwise!"

Pierre tried to collect his thoughts. He had to admit the man's reasoning wasn't far from the truth.

"That's possible," he conceded. "Let's just suppose that the Sea Gull did manage to arrange Françoise's return to Quimper. Then what? We're no further ahead. I'll ask you the same question I asked you before. What has any of this got to do with my relationship with Mireille?"

Farges perched sideways on the corner of the desk and slowly lit his cigarette.

"Well, at least we know one thing about the Sea

Gull: he wants to do some good for the Lachenaire children. He took it upon himself to bring Françoise back to Quimper and, at the same time, is trying to assure George's future. For George, the solution is very simple: he is to run the lab that once belonged to his father. Perrelet's letter makes that very clear."

"All right, now explain something for me. Why a letter to Perrelet and not to you?"

"Because our bird, like everyone else who writes anonymous letters, is a coward. He only attacks the weak: a young girl, an old scientist. . . . He'd never write to me; he's afraid of what my reaction would be!"

Pierre thought again about his Aunt Elise. If the Sea Gull thought of her as being weak, he was the only one who did! Farges went on talking.

"As for Françoise, he wants to find someone to take care of her, a marriage prospect, a man of means. In other words, a man like you."

"What? Are you telling me—?"

"Let me finish! I believe you *are* interested in her; I can see that the Sea Gull has cast his spell on you. You're the big winner; she's young and pretty. . . . The only trouble is that you're already involved with my daughter, who isn't bad either! There's even been talk of an engagement. . . . "

Pierre wanted to protest but Farges cut him off.

"Face it, my friend. Whatever your intentions might have been, that's where it's at!"

"Certainly not because of anything I did . . . or even said!"

"That's a matter of interpretation! When a man your age frequently sees a young woman from a good family, especially in a town like this—"

"To get to know each other, to find out if there was the possibility of things working out, we had to see each other once in a while! But I certainly never saw our relationship ending in marriage as a matter of course, like some kind of foregone conclusion!"

"In any case, the Sea Gull considered Mireille a serious obstacle to his plans for Françoise and he had to do something about her. That explains the letter she received at the restaurant."

Pierre was honest enough not to deny it. He couldn't help but give Farges credit for his intuition. The man did not have all the pieces, any more than Pierre did, but they had reached the same conclusion.

"You're probably right," concluded Pierre. "Now let me ask you a question. I know you're not the type of man to waste time in pointless chatter. What is the purpose of this conversation?"

"To help you see through this whole mess. I can't stand by and watch a man of your stature being manipulated like a puppet on a string!"

"Don't worry about me. I'm quite able to think for myself, and I'm free to make my own decisions. Let me emphasize that the Sea Gull had nothing to do with what you call my change of attitude toward Mireille. The letter only put into words what neither of us had been honest enough to admit. Furthermore, any decision I may make in the future will be my own, I can assure you."

Farges had a look of contempt on his face.

"Let's just say that you may be the only one who thinks so." He picked up the coat he had thrown over a chair when he had arrived and added, "Or at least, pretends to think so!"

Why bother to answer? Pierre couldn't be angry with Farges. Probably the man was only trying to help. He was glad Farges had come; he was now able to put things in their proper perspective. It had not been very pleasant, but it had been necessary, and he wanted Farges to know how he felt.

"I'm glad we had this discussion."

"I can't say the same. We don't seem to have gotten anywhere. I still don't understand why you insist on acting this way."

"Are you talking about Mireille? Please, let's not get into that again. Marriage shouldn't be arranged like a business deal."

"Funny how wrong a person can be. Until now, you gave me the impression that there were certain, let's say, business deals and sentimental attachments that were not unconnected."

"Are you referring to your last order?"

Pierre's best intentions were swept away in a moment of anger. Without waiting for an answer, he took a folder from his desk and pulled out a sheet of paper.

"Here it is. You can take it and tear it up!"

There were other things he could have said that would have been much more offensive, but Pierre managed to control his temper. The sheet of paper was trembling in his hand.

Startled for a second, Farges just shrugged.

"You are very touchy! I didn't mean to offend you. As a matter of fact, I thought I was paying you something of a compliment. Keep the order; nothing has changed."

Then he took on a more jovial tone. "If you turn it down, you'll be placing me in a rather difficult situation. You're the only one who can supply the containers by the time they're needed."

"All right. As long as we both understand that my business dealings with you have nothing to do with my seeing your daughter."

"Don't misunderstand me, I think it's too bad that you and Mireille . . . . But, I'll go on hoping. One of these days, common sense may prevail. I can't believe that you will allow yourself to be drawn in by this non-sense for very long."

"I'm not sure I know what you mean by nonsense, but believe me, I lead my own life!"

"Do you really think so? Just some advice, man to man: Françoise is obviously making a play for you. Don't be taken in. She's merely playing the role the Sea Gull has prescribed for her."

"You think she knows who the Sea Gull is?"

"Not only does she know, she's in on it with him!"

Pierre couldn't help but laugh.

"Quite original! I must admit I hadn't thought of it."

Farges did not show any signs of annoyance now. Standing by the door, his coat over his arm, he looked much as he did on other visits: the customer who becomes friendly again after the business talk is over. But Pierre could still see traces of resentment in his eyes.

"You couldn't possibly see the Lachenaire children from my point of view," Farges said. "They have never forgiven me for succeeding where their father failed. They want to get even with me and don't care what they have to do to accomplish it."

Before Pierre had a chance to protest, he continued, "You know, of course, that George is engaged?"

"Françoise told me that he was corresponding with a girl in Quimper."

"Didn't she tell you who? It's Dr. Guillou's daughter. And here's another thing that might interest you: George not only writes to her, he comes to see her. He's been seen on several occasions in the past few weeks. . . ."

Realizing that the conversation between the two men was nearly through, Mme Rogues quickly and silently moved away from the door and rushed to her chair. When Pierre and Farges appeared, she was typing furiously.

Chapter 13

When Pierre got home, Elise was sitting by the living-room window. She closed her book and looked at him in surprise.

"What are you doing here? I thought you were going to meet Françoise and the children on the beach!"

"I still have an hour. I want to talk to you first. I just had a discussion with Farges about the Sea Gull."

"Did he get a letter, too?"

"No, but his chemist did. You know, Perrelet. You were talking about him the other day. From what I could gather, it was a letter very much like yours."

"How did Farges find out?"

"I guess Perrelet told him."

"That would be proof of their complicity. But what does that have to do with us?"

"Farges is convinced that the Sea Gull is George Lachenaire."

Aunt Elise removed her glasses.

"Now, I've heard everything."

"That was my first reaction, too, but after finding out a few other things, I'm starting to wonder."

"What are you talking about?"

Aunt Elise didn't seem too impressed. Her expression was one of amused patience, like one who knew in advance that what was to follow would be complete nonsense.

"Oh, sit down. You're making me dizzy!"

"Where's Odile?"

"She's doing the children's room . . . and when are you going to stop smoking!"

Obediently, Pierre put his cigarette case back in his pocket and pulled up a chair.

"First of all, I should tell you that I've kept a few things from you."

Elise frowned and looked at him suspiciously. Before she could say a word, he went on.

"You seemed to attach so much importance to that anonymous letter that I didn't want to worry you."

"Tell me; then let me be the one to decide whether or not I should worry!"

"Okay. Here are all the events in the order that they happened—I've been trying to organize them in my mind on the way up here. Odile found your letter, Thursday, the twenty-eighth of March. That was the night I was having dinner with Mireille in Concarneau, remember? While we were having dessert, Mireille received a letter from the Sea Gull. It had been found on the porter's desk in the lobby."

"Why write to Mireille? To tell her about her father?"

"No, about me. To tell her that it would be a mistake for her to marry me."

"That suits me fine. Goes to show you that the Sea Gull isn't completely stupid!"

"Thanks a lot. Anyway, that same night, when I got home, I found another letter that someone had put in my coat pocket. It said basically the same thing as Mireille's: the Sea Gull told me it would be a catastrophe if I married her."

Pierre did not mention the part that dealt with Elise and the way she was raising the children. But, just as he expected, she asked to see the letter.

"Show it to me. I showed you mine."

"I . . . must have left it at the office. I'll try to remember to bring it to you. But listen, this is the interesting part of the story: it advised me to go to Paris the following Tuesday and be in the Saint-Germain-des Prés church at eleven o'clock in the morning."

"I recall that trip; you told me it was to meet a new customer from England."

"The truth is, it was to meet Françoise Lachenaire, but I didn't know it!"

"But you were supposed to have met by accident!"

"Françoise also received a letter. At least, that's what she told me."

"Have you any reason to think that's not true?"

Pierre's face registered uncertainty. Then he stood up, pulled the curtains apart and looked out to where the bright sunshine reflected like thousands of little emeralds on the lawn.

"Look!"

Elise raised her eyes and smiled. Perched on the porch outside was a sea gull.

"Odile will go out of her mind. It hasn't been here for several days. She was hoping it would never return."

"Does it come here often?"

"For some time, now, it's been perching there. The first time we noticed it was the day I received the letter! As far as Odile is concerned, it's a reincarnation of the devil! Mind you, there are some things about it that make you wonder. It's a very large gull of a species not common to this area."

"You're right; that type is usually found only on the high seas."

"I think it must be from the bird sanctuary at Cap Sizun. Could be it just comes to town once in a while for a change of scenery. Our property must be on its route, and it lands here to rest before going on."

"I think I like Odile's version better. Sometimes, I think we should believe more in fantasies. I was getting to the point of finding this whole affair quite marvelous, even miraculous! A great scheme to right a wrong and bring about true happiness for a few chosen people. . . . Now, I'm starting to wonder if it's not just a sordid little intrigue."

"My word, I think Farges has convinced you!"

"Let's just say that he has given me something to think about. He even suggests that Françoise is in league with her brother!"

"Maybe she is. It really doesn't seem to matter now. . . ."

"Well, I say no. It can't be true. She couldn't have fooled me to that extent!"

"What do you mean, 'fooled you'?"

"She was surprised when she saw me, when she recognized me or pretended to! Then later, when she was so happy at my suggestion that she come and spend some time here. Good Lord, the whole thing was probably planned!"

"Don't get carried away! This is silly. How could she have known you would invite her here? Your attitude is very strange, indeed. How can you let a crook like Farges do that to you . . . ?"

"One minute, his accusation makes sense, the next, it doesn't. I tell myself that George Lachenaire couldn't possibly be the Sea Gull, then I see that it couldn't be anyone else—"

"Now listen to me. Let's recap this whole situation. On one hand, there are arguments that say he is; on the other, arguments that say he isn't. You be the prosecutor, I'll act for the defense. You did the right thing in coming to see me; my book was starting to bore me, but this is getting really interesting."

"I wish I had your enthusiasm."

"I really don't see why you're reacting this way. Never mind. Let's examine the reasons that make you believe George Lachenaire is the Sea Gull."

"He's the one with the most to gain. Put yourself in his shoes. He's almost finished his studies; he's aware that Farges has robbed his family blind and decides to go after what he believes is his. But how? How can he prove that Farges is making his fortune from formulas perfected by his father, formulas that should have been part of his father's estate? He has no legal recourse. So, he decides to send anonymous letters to people who are aware of the circumstances and can do something to help him."

"First objection, of a psychological nature: George is a young man, just out of school. He has no experience as a scientist; it's quite unlikely that even he would think he would be able to carry out such an undertaking."

"Maybe not George, but his mother could. She might be the one who worked out all the details. By the way, I have a question to ask about that, a very important question. In his letter, the Sea Gull says that you witnessed certain things; in other words, you actually saw Farges come out of the lab that night. Now, how would he know that, unless he was there?"

"That's not impossible: a neighbor, a night watchman—"

"Come now! There's another possibility, a much more likely one. You probably told him, indirectly. Yes, you told Madame Lachenaire. Can you swear you never said a word about it?"

Looking away, Elise seemed to be going back several years. She was frowning. Pierre watched her anxiously.

"No," she said softly, "I couldn't swear to it. I really don't remember. We talked about so many things at the time!"

Pierre sighed and nodded his head.

"That's what I thought; there's no other explanation. Madame Lachenaire remembered what you told her and decided to refresh your memory, hoping you'd do something to help her. I'm sure she did the same thing with Perrelet."

"I have to agree that your reasoning makes sense. But only for those two letters. Why would Madame Lachenaire and her son be interested in your relationship with Mireille? What does Farges think about that?"

"He thinks the Sea Gull wanted to make me available for Françoise. I keep remembering the words, 'Above all, do not marry Mireille; she isn't meant for you!' Then it tells me to go to such-and-such a place at such-and-such a time, so I go there and find Françoise Lachenaire! It's pretty obvious, isn't it?"

"You mean George and his mother decided to kill two birds with one stone? Get back what Farges stole and marry off Françoise?" Elise started to laugh. "Pretty clever of them, isn't it? Funny, I always thought Madame Lachenaire was rather simple and not too bright! That plan has any number of loopholes. Think for a second of all the conditions required: that you go to Paris, that you drop Mireille, that you fall in love with Françoise, that you marry her. . . . Don't you think a lot of it is highly improbable?"

"But there's another detail: George Lachenaire was in

the church that day. I caught a glimpse of him in the shadows. He didn't even come out to say hello. When I asked Françoise about it later, she simply said he had come with her to make sure she would be safe."

"Well, I can see how that might be true!"

"But then, surely you can also see that he might have come to see if I had swallowed the bait!"

"All right, then. Let's go over the arguments that prove he couldn't be the Sea Gull. Until now, we have considered the motives rather than the facts. And facts are what count. We agree on one point: it seems logical for George Lachenaire to be the Sea Gull; but then it must also be practical for him to be the Sea Gull. He lives in Paris, right? How could he have delivered letters both here and in Concarneau?"

"Farges told me something rather interesting about that, too. George often comes here to see his fiancée. He is engaged, you see, to Dr. Guillou's daughter."

"That doesn't surprise me; when they were little, they were always together."

"On the twenty-eighth of March, three letters were hand-delivered here and one was mailed from Douarnenez to Françoise in Paris. If George was in the area that day . . . ."

"You are dealing in supposition, not facts. Just the same, I can find out for you."

"How?"

"By going to see Guillou. I have to see him anyway to get a new prescription for my rheumatism."

"I don't know when Perrelet received his letter, but while you're at it, try to find out if George was here the night Françoise arrived."

"Last Thursday? Why?"

"Remember the doorbell ringing around nine-thirty?"

"You told me nobody was there."

"So?" said Pierre. "Nobody was there, but the Sea Gull had come by and dropped a letter in the mailbox . . . if you can call it a letter! Just three words: 'Very well done!' written in the center of the page and, of course, the usual signature."

This time, Elise seemed astonished. She looked at her nephew, her face mirroring a combination of amazement, admiration and delight.

"How extraordinary!" she finally said. "You have to admit we are having an intriguing experience! Whoever he is, this Sea Gull is absolutely fascinating! He sees all, knows all and foresees all! He leads you by the nose and when you do what he says, he compliments you! A pat on the cheek for good little Pierre!"

"You may find it all very amusing, but I don't!"

"Why not? So little happens in this town. I am completely captivated by what's happening to us now, and I hope it goes on for a long time! But, let's get back to the Sea Gull. Suppose that George Lachenaire came to Quimper on the twenty-eighth of March. Explain to me how he could have put that letter on the mantel without anyone seeing him? Mind you, maybe he can go through walls. He seems to be able to do everything else!"

"He must have had someone to do it for him. Anything else would have been quite impossible."

"You mean Odile? But, you're the one who rejected that idea in the first place!"

"What about the gardener? He could have come in through the window, then raked the flower bed to get rid of his footprints."

Elise stopped. That possibility hadn't occurred to her. Then she raised an objection.

"That lout, that clumsy man, who doesn't have two words to say all day long? I've always thought he had rocks instead of a brain in his head!"

"A little bribe . . . ?"

"That's possible. Unlikely, but possible. But, how can you explain the letter in the restaurant?"

"Nothing simpler. I checked. It only took a second while the doorman was not in the lobby."

"But, the person would have to know ahead of time that you would be having dinner there!"

Now there was a valid argument. Pierre remembered that he had decided to go there at the very last moment. Only two people knew he would be there that night: his secretary and his aunt. He had called them as soon as he and Mireille had arrived, so they would know where to reach him in case of an emergency.

"We could have been followed," he suggested without much conviction.

Elise just shrugged without answering. After a moment's hesitation, he continued.

"Unless . . . . You're going to tell me again that I'm being absurd. I'm having a hard time trying to believe it, myself. But, listen. Guillou was in the restaurant that night. He went to the lobby to make a phone call at about the same time the letter was delivered."

Elise just rolled her eyes upward and sighed.

"Now it's Guillou! Why not the archbishop or the mayor? The Sea Gull is no longer a man or a woman; it's a whole group of people, a secret organization!"

At Pierre's look of complete discouragement, she continued, "Now you're upset! I realize that it seems like a strange coincidence, but really, can you see a man like Guillou getting mixed up in a thing like this? You can't really think he'd go around delivering anonymous letters just to please his future son-in-law! And how could he have known you'd be having dinner there? Really, Pierre, it just doesn't hold up!"

"Yet, the letters were typed by someone, delivered by someone. Until now, you've come up with only neg-

ative opinions. Let's suppose that George had nothing
to do with it. Then, who do you think the Sea Gull
could be?"

"I'm afraid that you're asking too much. It could
be anyone: a relative, a friend, one of Monsieur
Lachenaire's employees who was fired when Farges
took over the plant. . . . But why is it so important to
know the identity of the Sea Gull? Curiosity? Personally, I'm in no hurry. Life is usually awfully dull, so I'm
inclined to welcome anything that offers a little mystery! I'd like it to last as long as possible."

Pierre did not persist. It would be hard for him to tell
his aunt the true nature and reasons behind his curiosity. He really didn't care who the Sea Gull was, as
long as it was not George Lachenaire, as long as he
could be sure that Françoise had had nothing to do
with what had been happening. It had not required the
conversation with Farges for Pierre to ask himself that
question. It had crossed his mind in the church, and
until now, it had been easy to banish as quickly as it
came up. Its unlikelihood and absurdity made it seem
inoffensive. But now, Farges's arguments were giving it
some weight, and the idea began to gnaw relentlessly
at him.

Was Françoise working with the Sea Gull?

The revolt within him convinced Pierre of the full
power of his love. There was no doubt that he loved
Françoise with all his being, with all the tenderness
that had been preserved in his heart for so many
years—a heart as young and as free as that of a teenage
boy.

Farges's accusation had accomplished one thing; it
had forced Pierre to take a good long look at himself.
He realized his aloofness since Regine's death had pre-
vented him from really loving.

But it had also protected him from being hurt by

love. Now he knew that he had only two alternatives from which to choose: he could be happy . . . or he could be desperate.

As he left the house to meet Françoise and the children, Pierre was deeply troubled. The walk along the beach was to have been a happy one, but now it seemed like a test, a formidable test. He had made up his mind: one way or another, he would get the truth from Françoise. . . .

In just a few days, he had learned to read her face very well. The slightest trembling of her lips, the least quiver of her face held a meaning for him. He was positive he could tell whether she was innocent or guilty, simply by looking into her eyes. To him, Françoise was an open book.

Chapter 14

He saw them far off in the distance. They resembled three small insects against the vastness of sand and sea. He was pleased to be able to recognize them from so far away: he could even distinguish their individual silhouettes.

Françoise and Veronique were walking close together. Michel was a little ahead of them. With his red sweater, he reminded Pierre of a ladybird hopping at the water's edge.

He strode quickly down the windswept slope. From his position, he no longer could see civilization behind him. That world was cut off by the high cliffs. The scenery before him was reduced to two elementary arcs: the bay and the horizon, comprising nothing but sand, pebbles, water and hazy sky. Not a tree, not a house was in sight.

It was the season of high tides and, as it receded, the sea had not left one spot of dry sand; strands of algae lay plastered high up on the beach.

Michel saw his father first. Pierre watched as the ladybird changed into a running little boy with cheeks as red as his sweater. The boy jumped into his arms and hugged him.

"We built you a castle in the sand, big as this! And I collected a whole bunch of shells for you, too!"

Pierre thanked his small son with appropriate enthusiasm. The boy felt he had to give his father all the details.

"Françoise and I did most of the work! Veronique only gathered the algae for the garden."

"What garden?"

"The one we made in front of the castle. You'll see!"

A few minutes later, Pierre could hardly find the words to express his admiration of the medieval marvel, all fitted out with a moat, barbicans, half a dozen dungeons and several turrets.

"We weren't stingy with the materials or the manhours," said Françoise.

Her face was already tanned and expressed an almost childish joy; her eyes were the exact color of the sea. Like the children, she had removed her shoes, and sand clung to her legs. Seeing her looking so young, so radiant, made Pierre happy. His doubts seemed almost like an insult, and he had to repress an impulse to take her in his arms and ask her forgiveness.

"I was starting to worry," said Françoise, "I thought I might have taken the wrong turn and wound up at the wrong part of the beach."

"So was I. It wasn't too bright, asking you to meet me here. There is really no reference point and we could have been waiting for each other at opposite ends of the beach."

But now they were here.

"I haven't forgotten what you told me in Paris," he continued. "You wanted so much to see the beach and feel the wind. . . . I like this part of the beach the best, because of this simplicity. . . . Look at the sea and the sky. . . . "

He swept the horizon with his arm.

"See how rays of light bounce off the waves. It's a scene out of the Bible: the spirit of God above the abyss. . . . The earth has just been separated from the waters; it is still damp, undefined and uninhabited, sand and pebbles as far as the eye can see, the sky and the ocean still trembling from the shock of creation."

He stopped, slightly embarrassed. Françoise was smiling at him—not an ironic smile, but one filled with emotion. The children had wandered off, drawn by something at the water's edge.

"These wide open spaces cast a spell on me," he explained. "When I'm sad or simply tired, and sometimes, when I have a serious problem or have to make an important decision, I come here and walk in the wind, sometimes even in the rain. I think of nothing. I'm just an animal . . . less than an animal, a cell just emerging from the sea. . . . I return relaxed, regenerated, more lucid and confident."

Françoise had stopped smiling; she was listening to him very attentively, her eyes not leaving his face. They still held their tender expression, vaguely surprised, as if she were just discovering him. After some hesitation, she asked him a question.

"Did you choose this place for us to meet today because you have a particular problem you're worrying about?"

Pierre turned to look at his children who were happily chasing each other.

"I didn't have a problem when I made the suggestion. But this afternoon, I had a rather unpleasant visitor."

A look of anxiety crossed Françoise's face, but she did not ask any questions. Pierre thought that this would be a good time to say more, to tell her about Farges and his suspicions. She would not be expecting it. She would have no time to prepare herself. In her face, the slightest guilt would be quite obvious. But he did not have the courage . . . or, perhaps, the cowardice. He reassured her with a smile.

The spell has worked, he thought to himself. *I've forgotten my worries.*

His only desire was to prolong this moment, this feeling, so similar to what he had felt on the banks of the Seine, that first day. To him, this moment was more precious than the truth. He wanted only to stay there admiring the young woman against the backdrop of the restless sea, the oblique light and the wind playing sensuous games with her hair. One minute, a gust would whip it forward to mask her eyes or her lips, and the next, it would lift it to uncover the delicate lines of her neck.

The silence was overpowering. It was the kind of silence that follows a discovery or precedes a confession. Neither wanted to end it. They were united in some mystical happiness, struck by a spell that bound them together, still and peaceful.

It was as if the waves had carried Pierre's anguish out to sea. Who cared about the Sea Gull and his anonymous letters? Childish games! Did it really matter how he and Françoise had been brought together? Only one thing counted: they had met and Françoise was standing close to him in this world of sea and sky. . . .

En route to the beach, he had prepared all the questions that would have brought forth the truth. Now, they seemed senseless and futile. There was no truth more important than the delicate beauty of her face, which he wanted to cup in his hands.

His mind was filled with simple phrases, born of the profound tenderness in his heart, but a remnant of reason kept him from saying them: "You are as beautiful as the sea, soft as the light . . . I love you . . . I want only to take you in my arms. . . ."

Instead, he called up other words, his voice trembling as he spoke.

"Today, it is not just our surroundings that have cast the spell, but your being here. You have the power to chase the shadows. When I look at you everything becomes clear, and I can no longer believe in a lie."

Françoise looked at him the way a happy child looks at an adult who is sharing a confidence. When she spoke, it was with the timidity of a child.

"Why would you believe in a lie?"

Pierre brushed off the question with a vague gesture, saying it really didn't matter. Veronique and Michel returned just then and saved him from having to answer. The children were running around them, screaming so loudly they frightened the sea gulls perched some distance away.

Françoise became preoccupied by needs more immediate and pressing. She frowned when she saw Michel's feet; they looked as if he had been soaking them in an ink bottle. She managed to grab him as he flew past her.

"Let me look at your feet. Lift your leg. Well, you're a pretty sight! You've been playing in oil washed up on the beach. You even have some on your pants and sweater!"

"Very soon," said Pierre bitterly, "we'll have a sea of oil! With the garbage left by people and the oil spilled by ships, the beaches are turning into dumps!"

Michel did not seem too concerned. Perpetrator or victim, he looked at the results without much interest. Veronique, on the other hand, was quite upset.

"What will Aunt Elise say?"

Suddenly she noticed that her own legs and dress

were covered with black spots. Her face took on a hor-
rified expression.

"Françoise," she mumbled, "Françoise, look! It's all
over me too! That's terrible! I . . . I didn't even notice
it!"

She seemed terrified and her lips began to tremble.
Leaving Michel, Françoise went to her and tried to calm
her down.

"It was an accident, sweetheart. Don't worry about
it. We'll stop on the way back and buy some solvent.
We'll clean off the oil and you'll look as good as new."

Veronique, however, was not convinced; she looked
at her dress with an expression of dismay; she was
breathing fast and tears filled her eyes. Françoise continued to talk to her in a very calm voice, caressing her
hair, until she felt the child relax.

"Look at your brother," she said, laughing. "He's not
worried!"

"Oh him! The dirtier he is, the better he likes it!"

"That's not true, Veronique; he's just a boy, that's
all. Boys don't worry as much about such things. Go
and play some more with him."

When the child walked away, Françoise turned to
Pierre.

"There's a lesson to be learned from this. Veronique
appears to be very calm, but underneath she's extremely sensitive. The slightest little thing takes on
huge proportions. We must try to show her the need
not to get too upset; if we don't, she may cause herself
a lot of needless suffering as she grows up."

"I have already noticed a change in her since you've
been here. She has confidence in you and she listens to
you; you show her what is important and what is not.
That's one thing Aunt Elise never knew how to do."

"Don't speak badly about your aunt. She may have
her faults, but she means well."

"I don't mean to criticize her. I have a lot of affection for Aunt Elise and certainly I'm grateful to her. But I can't help deploring some of her attitudes toward the children. And I don't seem to be able to make her understand."

"I think it's because she doesn't have enough time. Looking after the house is a major task."

"It's her own fault that she doesn't have enough time. She could hire help, but she can't get along with anybody, and nobody can put up with her for long, except Odile!"

Françoise was smiling, but she looked as though she didn't believe him. He hastened to add, "And now there's you, of course. I don't know how you've done it, but I've even noticed a few changes in Elise herself, since you've been here!"

"Simply because I'm taking part of the load off her shoulders. She seems to be more understanding of the children because she doesn't have to look after them all the time. And I must say that the rapport between us has been very good!"

Françoise glanced at her watch.

"Let's not spoil things by being late for dinner. We'd better start back."

Pierre's reaction was that of a child whose playtime had just been cut short.

"Already? I haven't been here any time at all!"

"I don't drive as fast as you do, and don't forget that we have to stop along the way; operation cleanup!"

"I was hoping we could take a long walk along the beach; I have so many things to tell you."

He looked very disappointed; Françoise put her hand on his arm.

"We'll come back. Aunt Elise is very strict about us being on time for meals, and I can understand it—she's the one who does the cooking. Let's not risk spoiling her meal, even if it seems like a small thing to us. People attach such importance to details."

Her voice was serious and quite persuasive. Pierre couldn't help laughing as he spoke.

"You sound about a hundred years old. I feel like a little boy who has to be convinced to do the right thing."

"You're not far off! I hope you're not going to act up in front of the children!"

"Don't worry. Now I know why they behave so well and are so happy with you at the same time."

"Maybe it's because I'm happy with them."

Pierre almost said, "Then you must never leave them." But the same small voice of logic inside his head kept him from uttering a word. It was not because he thought he should tread carefully; it was more a kind of superstitious fear, the feeling that he couldn't let himself go until he knew the identity of the Sea Gull. Somehow, that seemed to be the price he was expected to pay for happiness. . . .

Turning away from the sea, he took the young woman's hand and led her toward the road.

On their way back, Pierre following Françoise's car, they stopped at a little grocery store to buy the cleaning fluid. They were greeted by a woman in traditional costume.

"Why don't you clean up your children here, madame? You'll be much more comfortable," she suggested.

Françoise didn't flinch at being called madame, but she avoided Pierre's eyes. His eyes, however, never left her face as she proceeded to clean up Veronique and Michel. The simplicity of the scene troubled him because of its simplicity—the everyday gestures of maternal care. He had completely forgotten how tender and precise they could be. In this humble setting, they took on the very meaning of life.

These were scenes that, no matter what happened, Pierre could never forget: the young woman in her simple dress, with her soft voice and the face of a child, his children who seemed to be discovering their own identities, and this country grocery store where the smells of many varied products mingled. . . .

"Papa, will you buy us something?"

Being nice to someone can sometimes bring great reward. No village storekeeper ever made better sales in midafternoon: a toy car, a china doll, half a pound of candies, a lace apron for Aunt Elise, some embroidered slippers for Françoise. . . .

Françoise felt she should stop Pierre. He seemed intent on buying everything in the store.

"If I had known cleaning up the children would be so expensive . . . !"

He was laughing, happy with his purchases. Veronique was soon without a trace of oil or worry, and she thanked Françoise in her own way. She took hold of her hand and smiled at her as if to say: "You were right. You're always right . . . I love you very much. . . ."

As for Michel, he made such a fuss about being separated from Françoise that Veronique offered to ride home in her father's car.

"I can't very well let you drive by yourself, after you bought me a new doll."

Pierre was a little upset, even a little jealous, at first.

"Am I to understand that you're driving home with me only out of politeness and a sense of duty?"

"Of course not! It's just that you're a man, and we don't have much in common to talk about!"

"Oh, really? I hope for your sake you change your mind some day, or else you'd better forget about getting married!"

A little while later, pointing to the small car in front of them, he asked her if she was getting along all right with Françoise. The little girl blurted an enthusiastic "yes" without the slightest hesitation.

"Would you like it if she stayed with us always?"

Veronique didn't answer, but when Pierre turned to look at her, he saw in her eyes a mixture of curiosity and hope. He knew she was stuck on the word "stay." Perhaps, she had expected him to say more, because when her father did not continue, she said, with such fervor that her voice trembled, "I don't want her to leave! Even when the holidays are over!"

"That's not up to us, my darling. Have you told her?"

"Yes."

"And what did she say?"

"That it wasn't up to her. . . . "

Meanwhile, Michel was wasting no time making his feelings known to Françoise.

"You know, I'm really glad you're here. Papa is, too!"

"Are you sure? How can you tell?"

"Well, for one thing, he never comes to meet us when Aunt Elise takes us to the beach."

Françoise was trying to see Pierre's face in her rear-view mirror. All she could see was the reflection of the sun on his windshield. She smiled at him anyway, as if he could see her. There was a pause before Michel continued.

"Do you know what Veronique told me on the beach, a little while ago? But she made me promise not to tell you. So you have to promise you won't tell her I told you!"

"There's something not quite right about all this, but okay, I promise."

"She told me that papa should marry you, and then you would be our mother, and you wouldn't leave and we could go to the beach or the country every day."

Françoise was not able to respond. The emotions brought on by the boy's simple words had choked her.

"I would like that very much," Michel whispered seriously. Unfortunately, he couldn't stop there and began to elaborate.

"I would rather have you than Mireille."

"Mireille Farges?"

"Yes. Do you know her? Of course, she's pretty too, but not as pretty as you. And she's not any fun. She never knows what to say to us, and I think we just annoy her."

Françoise hesitated, torn between the desire to know more and the shame of taking advantage of a child's innocence. "Do you think . . . that . . . your father wants to marry her?"

"I don't know. I've seen them kissing, sometimes, but— What's the matter? Are you angry? Oohh . . . I shouldn't have said that!"

Françoise forced a smile.

"Why not, Michel? What's so special about that? Your father kisses Aunt Elise every night."

"That's not the same. Did my father ever kiss you?"

"That's really none of your business. You're asking silly questions now!"

Françoise shrugged in a gesture of exasperation. She spoke more harshly than she intended when Michel opened his mouth to say more.

"That's enough, Michel!"

The boy looked surprised. She had never spoken to him in that tone of voice. But he got the message and scrunched himself in the corner of the seat, sucking his thumb like a baby, always his reaction when he was sad and confused.

Françoise felt her heart swell with tenderness—a tenderness that quite suddenly was very painful. Her eyes glistened.

Chapter 15

Farges's confident statement to Pierre that the Sea Gull would never dare attack him couldn't have been further from the truth. That same night, he received an anonymous letter, marked "Personal."

He had stayed quite late at his office to examine some layouts for an advertising campaign, which had just been completed by an agency in Paris. The clock showed almost eight when he decided to call it a day. The lateness of the hour didn't prevent him from making his usual rounds; he couldn't leave without checking things over.

He noticed as he went by there were no lights on in the lab. Unlike his boss, Perrelet had been leaving earlier the past few days. That business with the letter had certainly affected him.

The cleaning staff had started to work on the main floor. Instead of acknowledging their greeting, Farges shouted, "Don't forget to turn the lights off!" An uneasiness settled over him when he remembered the night watchman didn't always come in before they were gone.

His rounds didn't take more than five minutes. When he returned to his office, the letter was resting against his briefcase. He recognized the typed words right away. A wave of fear washed over him.

Before opening the envelope, he looked into the adjoining room, which he used for staff meetings. It was empty. There was nobody in the hallway either. He rushed to the window, but the lot was deserted.

In front of him, through the window of a house attached to the right of the entrance, he could see, in the light from a television set, his handyman sitting at the table, having dinner with his family.

One of the cleaning women? Farges would certainly have met her on the stairs or in the hallway. That was highly unlikely, in any case. He could only conclude that someone had come into the plant before the workers had gone home—someone who would have to be still on the premises.

Farges picked up the phone and called the handyman. He saw him get up from the table while his wife lowered the sound on the television.

"Are the gates closed?"

"As usual, monsieur, they are closed as soon as the workers go home."

"The back door too?"

"It's never open. Besides yourself and me, no one has a key."

"Are you sure?"

"Absolutely . . . unless you gave yours to someone. . . ."

"Think hard; there are no other exits out of this plant at this moment?"

There was silence. The man must have been wondering why all the questions.

"I can assure you, monsieur . . . I really don't see . . . unless someone went through my kitchen or over the fence. . . . "

"Very well, go back to your dinner. I may need you in a little while."

After hanging up, Farges kept his hand on the receiver. Should he call the police and have the plant searched? What reason should he give?

If the Sea Gull was cornered, he might become violent. Perhaps he should have the handyman accompany him? No. Better not to involve anyone else.

Farges had almost forgotten about the letter. Opening it he found two sheets of paper. One was a photocopy of a document filled with numbers and formulas. He recognized it immediately and turned white as a sheet. Then he looked at the letter; from the very first word, his face expressed anger.

On Tuesday, February 17, 1973, at 9:45, you went into the lab by way of the back door. You "borrowed" the New Products file from Maurice Lachenaire's safe. The death of Lachenaire a few hours later must have upset you so much that you forgot to return it at the time the estate was being probated.

And so, today, with the complicity of your chemist you profit from formulas that really belong to Mme Lachenaire.

It would be advisable to clear up this situation before it is made public. Scandal should be avoided if possible. You are very aware of your position and pleased with your success; therefore you would be well advised to follow the two suggestions below:

Reinstate Mme Lachenaire in her rightful place by giving her back the shares that were fraudulently taken from her.

Hire her son as the head of scientific and technical research. You may continue to manage the financial aspects and the administrative functions and keep, if you so desire, the title of Chairman of the Board.

By doing so, you will be considered very generous by the people of Quimper.

If you refuse, you will regret it.

—The Sea Gull

P.S. A small detail that may encourage you to act positively on the above suggestions: there were several copies of the formulas contained in the New Products file.

Enclosed, please find a photocopy of one of these documents, dated and signed by Maurice Lachenaire.

Chapter 16

The Sea Gull was becoming set in his ways. The doorbell rang at precisely the same time as it had for the previous evening delivery.

Pierre was working in his small office on the ground floor of the house. At least, he was trying to concentrate on the work he had brought from the plant. Only eight days earlier, he almost enjoyed going through the reports and cost sheets; now, it bored him. He used to become very impatient with himself whenever he wasted time. Now, he had the feeling that, by working so late, he was wasting the most precious time of his life.

It had been a lost evening. In an obvious departure from the pattern established since her arrival, Françoise had gone to her room right after putting the children to bed.

"I'm rather tired," she had apologized. "We did so much running around at the beach today."

"I hope you haven't caught a cold," Pierre had said, concern in his voice. "You probably shouldn't have stayed so long in the wet sand in your bare feet."

Taking her hand, he had tried to look into her eyes, but was surprised when she had turned away, with a simple good night.

He had noticed during dinner that she had said very little and her smile appeared forced. And more than once he saw that her eyes had a questioning look, mingled with a tender sadness. He had tried to find out what had brought about this sudden change in attitude, but to no avail.

To Elise, there was only one explanation. And soon as she was alone with him, she started right in to tell him a thing or two.

"What did you say to her? I suppose you told her what Farges said!"

"I never mentioned a word."

"Thank God for that. At least you've come around to my way of thinking! I just couldn't understand an intelligent man like you giving any kind of credence to the blatherings of a man like Farges!"

"Let's understand each other, Aunt Elise. I think the same way you do only when I'm with Françoise. Or rather, I pretend to think like you, because what might be the truth scares me and I would rather not face it. But the minute I'm alone, all the doubts creep back and I come back to the same conclusion: of all the possibilities, the most likely one is the one involving the Lachenaire family."

Pierre had restlessly paced the living room. Sitting in her armchair, Elise had stared at him in astonishment and disbelief.

"I totally disagree with you," she said. "The Sea Gull is only the master of ceremonies, a puppeteer, holding the strings of his marionettes . . . but how could he possibly manipulate them from a distance?"

She had paused, then continued talking as if she were thinking out loud.

"Among other things, he would have to live in Quimper and be in a position that allows him to keep a close watch on the events and actions, even the thoughts, of his characters."

Suddenly her tone changed.

"It really doesn't matter. I have no intention of getting into another discussion like the one we had this afternoon. I'm sleepy and I'm going to bed. Good night."

She had virtually flown from her chair, kissed him and rushed to the door, as though she had suddenly realized something was burning on the stove. . . .

Now, at the sound of the doorbell, Pierre jumped but made no attempt to answer the door. Instead, he rushed to the window. He had a hard time getting it open, it was several seconds before he was able to climb through it and leap into the garden. He dashed toward the gate, opened it and ran into the street. . . .

He saw no one.

He was tempted to keep running, but in what direction? The Sea Gull had had enough time to make his escape.

This time, there were two envelopes in the mailbox: one addressed to him, the other to Françoise.

Françoise had not yet closed her shutters and the light was still on. Pierre stopped, fascinated by the rectangle of light. Did she know he was outside, watching her window? He saw her silhouette and stood staring, all the while fighting the impulse to cry out. He wanted to shout, tell her he loved her. . . . But she couldn't have seen him—the curtains were closed.

There was no light in Aunt Elise's room. She was probably already asleep. Pierre climbed back in through the window, this time ruining the flowers that were just starting to grow.

Now he was angry and the letters trembled in his hands. This time, the Sea Gull had gone too far; the joke had gone on long enough. It wasn't funny anymore. How long would he keep pulling the strings?

Pierre did not find the comparison to marionettes particularly pleasing, but had to admit it was apt. As he read, the comparison became even more appropriate.

Love takes from men the reasoning it gives to women. Here are a few suggestions that may keep you from doing something stupid:

1. George Lachenaire is not the Sea Gull. To prove it, he is in Paris at this very moment, as this letter is being delivered to you. You can call him if you need to convince yourself.

2. Françoise doesn't know any more than you do.

3. You love her. She loves you. She is ideal for your children, and they adore her. She even won over your Aunt Elise.

What are you waiting for?

—The Sea Gull

Pierre read the letter several times, his face wiped clean of any sign of irritation. A burst of joy rushed through his whole body.

"Françoise doesn't know any more than you do. . . . She loves you. . . . " In two short sentences his burden was lifted. Not for a second did he doubt their accuracy. He accepted them blindly and was given complete peace of mind.

Something had been bothering him, and tonight, it became almost frightening: how could the letter have the answers to questions that had been troubling him for only the past few hours? Unless one believed in ESP or subscribed to some other parapsychological phenomenon. . . .

Could it be pure coincidence? The Sea Gull had already proven his ability to foresee the reactions and feelings of his characters. One could assume that the letters were written in advance; yet they always arrived at the most opportune time and made a maximum impact. Aunt Elise had stated it very clearly a short while ago: "The Sea Gull must be in a position that allows him to keep a close watch on events and actions of his characters. . . . "

Deep in thought, he remained motionless, staring at the phone. He reached it and snatched up the receiver, quickly dialing a number.

'Madame Rogues's number. . . . "

Listening to the phone ring at the other end, Pierre's heartbeat increased and his breathing became faster. His secretary, the Sea Gull! It hadn't dawned on him before. Elise's words had brought it home to him. Mme Rogues was aware of Pierre's every move, his dealings with Farges, with Mireille; she knew everything about his professional and personal life. She was the one in whom he confided, and the only one who could have known of the afternoon's conversation.

The arguments that pointed to her were rushing through his head. He remembered giving her an old typewriter no longer being used in the office. She owned a car. After work, she had all the free time in the world.

And tonight . . . Living as she did on the other side of town, Mme Rogues would not have had time to get home. If she didn't answer . . . .

A small click and Pierre's theory crumbled. He recognized her sleepy voice at the other end of the line.

Mme Rogues was not the Sea Gull. Suddenly the whole situation became intolerable. Pierre did not feel like talking to her, and he dropped the receiver back into its place.

He went up the stairs, walked toward Françoise's room and knocked lightly on her door. She opened it.

"Françoise, excuse me, but I noticed from downstairs that you were still up. I have a letter for you."

"A letter at this hour?"

She thought he was joking, but her eyes dropped to the envelope in his hand. She took it and raised it to the light.

"The Sea Gull," she whispered.

"Yes, I got one too." Pierre watched her anxiously, as she read the few lines.

The light created a halo around her hair. He noticed that her hand was trembling and asked her, his voice quaking, if the letter bore good or bad news. She seemed very serious and there was curiosity in her look.

Pierre realized the reason for her hesitation; it was not up to her to break down the barrier that stood between them.

Choosing what seemed to be the most practical solution, he took his own letter from his pocket.

"The Sea Gull doesn't have much confidence in me. He probably thinks I won't tell you what he has written. There was a time when he might have been right. I know I am feeling something, and I know it is exceptional, probably something I'll never be able to feel again. At my age, people are inclined to doubt what is right before their eyes. Yet we know the danger of losing sight of what is truly meaningful—the danger of losing something forever. And, when something really important happens, we put off saying anything because of doubts, fear of saying the wrong thing. And then, one day, it is too late—too late ever to know what real happiness is. The Sea Gull is trying to protect me against myself. He is forcing me to speak . . . to act. Here, read this and you'll understand. Or do you already know?"

Françoise nodded. "Let's trade," she suggested. "You'll see that the Sea Gull has done it again. Our letters are probably very similar."

The two letters changed hands. Pierre quickly scanned the one he now held.

No matter what you hear about Mireille Farges, don't pay any attention. Pierre never thought of her as more than a passing fancy.

On the other hand, if you knew how to read what was in his eyes, you would know what was in his heart. He loves you. And if you would look into yourself, you would see that you love him too.

Why wait? It is never too soon to be happy!

                                      —The Sea Gull

Pierre stared at the letter for a few moments, then folded it; his eyes met hers. She had also finished reading. He knew the Sea Gull was right. Françoise was smiling in a way he had never seen her smile before. No, to call it a smile was not quite accurate; the muscles of her face had not moved. Rather, there was a kind of glow about her, visible on the outside, but originating from deep within.

He drew her close and wrapped her in his arms. Her head rested against his chest. She stayed there for a long moment, clinging to him, breathing in deep sighs as though she had finally come to the end of a long and difficult journey. Gradually, she began to relax in this newly discovered refuge of strength and tenderness.

"My love," whispered Pierre, trailing kisses along her cheek and neck, "My precious love . . . I have waited for so long, without even knowing it. I would never have believed this could be possible. I have not been living; I have just been letting my life slip away, day after day, like the sand on the beach washing away with the tide. All it took was a turn of my head to see the light in your hair, the smile in your eyes, in the shadowy silence of a church, for me to realize that I had been waiting for you. In that instant, I knew the reason for my desperate loneliness. I was without you. . . ."

She pulled back slightly and gazed into his face. Her eyes, so near now, seemed very large and luminous in the semidarkness of the hallway.

"I was terrified," she confessed. "The moment I saw you, I knew my life could never be the same again. . . . Pierre, I have to tell you something. Your face, your voice, the way you smile . . . all these things have always been a part of me, even though they were buried somewhere deep in my memory. I remember the way you looked at me especially the day of my father's funeral. You offered friendship, and oh, such tenderness. . . . These are images I have kept secret."

Seeing the love in his face, Françoise reached up and put her arms around his neck, drawing him close to her.

At the other end of the hallway, a door closed slowly and silently.

Chapter 17

"Ahead, a little more . . . more . . . more. . . . There! That's good. Well done! The car will be just fine here."

Pierre grinned.

"A little too well done, maybe. I'll probably never be able to get it out."

Françoise had asked him to drive her to a very narrow track in the heart of a fir forest. Her reason had been somewhat oblique.

"I don't want us or the car to be seen from the road, you see."

Pierre didn't have a clue as to what this was all about, but he had promised not to ask any questions.

"Come, we can cut across this field."

They returned on foot to the road, followed it for a short distance, then turned right onto a path that wound its way through bullrushes. The sea was very near, a metallic surface shining in a luminous vapor. It was the beginning of May and the tall grass foretold the coming of summer.

"You have to admit I picked a beautiful day . . . but, to tell you the truth, this isn't really the place I had in mind. . . ."

She watched Pierre from the corner of her eye, waiting for the question she knew he would eventually ask. Despite his efforts to appear indifferent, he cast worried looks in her direction more and more often. The more disturbed he looked, the more she laughed, which did nothing to reassure him.

This game—and it was a game—had started the previous evening. Françoise had come to pick up Pierre at the plant.

"Tell me quickly if you think you can take tomorrow afternoon off."

"Why not? Lately, as you may have noticed, I've been taking more and more time off!"

He had glanced at his agenda. Two meetings of no particular importance. Mme Rogues could reschedule both of them without any trouble. Nonetheless, until a month ago, he had very rarely left his office in the middle of the day. Although he felt like a boy playing hooky from school, he had no regrets. Business had carried on normally during his absences from the office. He was learning to rely more on his associates, and they, in turn, were happy to have the opportunity to take on more responsibility.

"Do you want to go somewhere?"

"Yes . . . but you mustn't ask any questions. It's a surprise!" Françoise smiled at her secret.

To add to the mystery, she had asked him not to mention a word to anyone.

"After lunch," she had said, "leave the house and go back to the office as usual. I'll pick you up around three."

Pierre had been mystified from the very beginning. Françoise had arrived exactly on time, carrying a rectangular parcel under her arm. A gift for someone?

"First of all, we'll go to Douarnenez. Then, we'll follow the coastline until we reach Cap Sizun."

Still no explanation. And the smile was the same as the night before. Pierre was happy to go along, even though he felt a little foolish taking part in what seemed to be a childish game. With her pink cheeks and sparkling eyes, Françoise was obviously having a wonderful time. Along the way, she had given him some astonishing news.

"Mother will be here in two days. You'll never believe why!"

"She's coming to see me, so she can hug me and tell me how happy she is because I'm going to be her son-in-law. . . ."

"That, too . . . but that's only part of it. Listen to this! She got a letter from Farges!"

Pierre stopped in his tracks.

"I told you you wouldn't believe it! He wants to talk to her about transferring part of the business back to her. She quoted his exact words: ' . . . in view of certain technicalities, which I would like to discuss with you . . . .' "

Quite casually, Pierre started walking again, trying his best not to display the slightest sign of surprise. It was his turn to have one up on Françoise. He was so convincing, she asked, "Aren't you the least bit surprised?"

"Not really. In fact, I think its something we might have expected. Obviously, Farges has received a letter from the Sea Gull. Did he give any reason for this sudden burst of generosity?"

"Fate— No, seriously! Fate has allowed him to get hold of certain formulas. He claims that, in all fairness, they should have been considered part of the estate and—"

"Beautiful! That letter must be a masterpiece! I hope Aunt Elise gets a chance to read it."

"So do I. She'll certainly be interested. . . . But that's not all. Farges is also going to offer George a job. He's to be trained to take over the lab. Certainly, it's a good time for it. Perrelet has been thinking of retiring."

"Your brother must be delighted."

"He doesn't want any part of it."

In spite of himself, Pierre looked astonished.

"He turned it down flat," Françoise went on. "Mother is absolutely furious!"

"Well, I can understand how she would be. It seems foolish not to—"

"You don't know George. In the first place, he can't stand the thought of working with Farges. But the main reason is that he just isn't interested in doing research in cosmetics. He'd rather set up a medical lab with Dr. Guillou."

"For the first time," Pierre remarked thoughtfully, "the Sea Gull is wrong. One of his characters doesn't want to follow through." Then, after a pause, he asked, "Is that the surprise you wanted to tell me about?"

Françoise shook her head, and her smile broadened.

At last they reached the crest of the bluffs. On one side were the cliffs, on the other, rolling hills. Beyond was the naked sea.

"This is it."

It was the most remote spot on the coast, a small plateau covered with moss and accented by a pyramid-shaped pile of wood, which had probably served as a reference point for seamen. The road ended abruptly at the edge of the cliff, and a hundred feet below the waves crashed against the rocks.

"Let's go a little farther on."

Pierre followed her, somewhat resigned by this time, and simply enjoyed the sights and sounds of nature at its savage best. They crouched behind a large rock. Françoise was still clutching the parcel. Suddenly, she handed it to him.

"This is where the surprise begins!" she announced. "You may look at it, now."

It was a book entitled, *The Wonders of Nature*. Pierre recognized it right away. It was an illustrated encyclopedia he had bought for Veronique a few years before, now enriched with Michel's own illustrations.

"What's this?"

He looked so disappointed that Françoise took pity on him. Trying not to laugh, she told him that the answer to the puzzle was inside the book.

"Let it fall open by itself."

Pierre did as she instructed and the pages began to part; the book stayed open at a page illustrated with birds.

"Now you know why we're here!"

"I do? Françoise, I haven't the slightest idea what any of this is about! In fact, I'm beginning to wonder if maybe I'm not just plain stupid!"

"We're sea-gull hunting. Look!"

Raising her arm, she pointed to the west, where a jetty stretched out into the ocean like the prow of a destroyer.

"See that point? It's the bird sanctuary at Cap Sizun. There, you can find petrels, penguins, pelicans, albatrosses . . . and sea gulls! If everything goes well, we should be able to see some any minute."

She tapped her finger on the book.

"Meanwhile, I thought it would be a good idea for us to read about some of their characteristics. Look at this one. . . . "

She was pointing to an illustration of a sea gull. Startled, Pierre leaned forward to take a closer look. There was no mistaking it; he recognized the picture immediately. It was a sea gull, exactly the size of the one that had been used as a signature on the letters! He also noticed that the illustration seemed to stand out in slight relief. Someone had used it many times to trace the outline of a sea gull. Françoise looked at him with amusement.

"Feel better about your state of mind now? What about mine? I found that book a few days ago at the back of a closet. I flipped through it without paying much attention at first; then I saw that illustration. I can tell you right now that neither Michel nor Veronique traced the outline of that bird. I asked them!"

"Aunt Elise?"

Françoise gestured as if to say, "Who else?"

Pierre started to stand up, but Françoise held him back.

"Don't move. And for heaven's sake be quiet!"

"Why?"

"Because we're keeping watch and we don't want to be discovered. We'd scare them off! It's almost time. . . ."

"Aunt Elise . . . " he kept repeating, as though trying to convince himself of the outrageous possibility. "Aunt Elise, the Sea Gull!"

"Incredible, isn't it?"

"Yes . . . then again, no. The idea occurred to me once or twice, but I immediately put it out of my mind. It was just too ridiculous! And yet, when you stop to think about it, it's really quite logical. Aunt Elise certainly qualifies! She was in a position to know all the necessary facts about all of the people the Sea Gull has been trying to help."

"Yes. I believe she transferred the affection she used to have for my father to my family. She knew we had been victimized, and she felt she should try to do everything she could to make things right."

"Well, I guess she's pretty fond of me, too. She knew it would be a bad mistake for me to marry Mireille Farges. She had to find a way to break it up and steer me in your direction. She certainly didn't get into this thing for herself. She didn't care what we thought of her, as long as we didn't suspect her. Oh, she's been having a grand old time, though. Can you imagine the laugh she must have had when I told her I was going to Paris on business? And remember the day I went to the beach to meet you and the children? Before I left, I spent at least half an hour with her, telling her all about the letters she'd been writing!"

Pierre couldn't help smiling at the irony of it all. "And to think she had the gall to ask me to show her the letter that called her an old shrew."

Françoise was smiling too, but her expression was quite different, more tender, filled with affection. She rested her head against Pierre's shoulder.

"I suspected her the first night I arrived. It was more intuition than anything else, but there was something about her attitude toward me, and the, well, mocking way she would look at you when you weren't watching. I thought right away that she was playing some kind of game and having a lot of fun while she was at it!"

"I never noticed a thing. But, thinking back, I can see now that I should have figured it out from the very first letter!"

"How come?"

"Well, I reacted just the way Odile did. I became fascinated by the mystery of it. A letter arrives and no one knows how. All the windows are locked, all the doors are locked. . . . If I had used my head for a minute, I would have realized right away that Aunt Elise was the

only one who could have possibly put the letter there.
All she had to do was double back, come in through
the laundry-room door and put the letter on the mantel, when Odile was in the kitchen. Then, she could go
out and come back later, after she had done her shopping. Mind you, I still haven't figured out how she
could have delivered the other letters, herself."

"There's only one answer to that!"

"I know. Someone else delivered them. But, I just
can't see it. Knowing her as I do, I can't imagine her involving anyone else."

"Unless the 'anyone else' happens to be the Sea
Gull. . . ."

"What?"

"Wait. Listen. . . ."

Françoise lifted her head; something had caught her
attention. She peered cautiously down the road they
had taken.

"I won't have to tell you any more," she whispered.
"You'll see for yourself in a minute."

She squeezed his hand.

"Don't make a sound! Don't even breathe! They
mustn't know we're here!"

The sound of a car approaching drowned out the
wind and sea. An old black car bounced up and down
on the road. Françoise looked at Pierre and he nodded
his head to say he understood everything now. He slid
his arm around her waist and put his lips close to her
ear.

"What are they doing here? And why bring the car
this far ?"

"We'll soon find out."

Elise was the first to get out of the car. She was
dressed far more casually than usual: gray skirt, tailored white blouse. Her face was beaming; she looked
ten years younger.

The door on the other side of the car opened and Perrelet appeared. He also looked different from his usual self: shirt open at the neck, beige pants and a rust-colored jacket. More than anything, he resembled an elderly student, but this time, the student was on holiday.

Against the luminous sky, the two presented an extraordinary illusion of youth. One could easily imagine them as they might have been thirty or forty years before, dressed much the same way, doing almost the same thing. They would have moved closer to each other—as they were doing now—and each would place an arm around the waist of the other—as they were doing now. . . .

Pierre was not alone in his astonishment. Françoise squeezed his hand even more, her lips parted and her eyes sparkled as she witnessed the aging lovers in this setting of romance and grandeur, surrounded by the flowers of spring and the cliffs of unyielding granite.

There was tenderness and confidence in their every gesture. They were silent, clinging to each other as they looked out to sea. The wind played in their hair, revealing relentless white, while the sun with kindlier warmth found a strand or two of gold. . . .

What followed was equally astonishing. Perrelet strode to the trunk of the car and lifted out a large box. Aunt Elise spoke a few words to him; he appeared to agree and put the box on the ground. He lifted something out of it that, judging by the expression on his face, must have been quite heavy. Françoise and Pierre could see that it was a very old typewriter. They immediately realized the purpose of this trip.

"Be careful!" cautioned Elise.

Perrelet staggered to the edge of the cliff.

"I can see it all now! The way you're going, you'll

end up at the bottom of the cliff and leave me stuck here with that old piece of junk!"

Behind the boulder smiles were exchanged. Elise would always be Elise. Love had not changed her.

There was the sound of crashing metal . . . and gradually it faded away. The old machine tumbled from rock to rock, smashing into a thousand pieces that scattered at the bottom of the cliff. The sea would keep its secret.

Pierre looked at Françoise. Her eyes were filled with tears.

"I'm just being silly," she whispered, her voice breaking.

"No, you're not," he murmured, for he also was quite touched. That old machine, having typed its few letters, had been the instrument that had brought them happiness. . . .

A sudden fright stopped them from becoming too sentimental. Perrelet was no longer in sight! Surely, he couldn't have . . . . But no, there he was, behind his car, closing the trunk. He lit a cigarette and looked out over the bay, where white and blue sails glided in the wind.

It was obvious that he wanted to stay longer, to sit on one of the huge rocks, close to Elise, and simply enjoy the surroundings.

But Elise, clearly impatient, was signaling to him to hurry. She was emphasizing her words with unmistakable gestures. Pierre didn't have to hear her to know what she was saying. She was prattling about a dinner to prepare . . . a washing to do . . . the children coming home from school before she got back and Françoise out for the whole afternoon. . . . At the temptation of a peaceful stay, she hurled the virtue of her housework.

Perrelet surrendered. They climbed in the car and headed straight for the cliff. Cold sweat ran down Pierre's back.

"What if he comes this far to make his turn?"

The ground sloped toward the sea; the grass was very slippery. Even with a good car it would be risky; with that old relic, it was suicide!

A second's pause, then two sighs of relief. The old car ground into reverse and, guided by the ruts in the road, traveled backward at full speed, like a train on its tracks. Stunned and choked with emotion, Françoise and Pierre shared the illusion that they were watching an old movie running backward . . . back, back into the past.

When the car was out of sight, they both wondered if they had actually witnessed a real scene. Or had it all been a dream and now time itself was running backward, in order to wipe it all out . . . ?

"There . . . " sighed Françoise.

They sat on the grass, where just a few minutes before, Elise and Perrelet had held each other close. Françoise leaned back to rest against Pierre, her arms on his arms, her face against his. The perfect seat. It breathed when she breathed and gave her light kisses every few seconds . . . Unfortunately, it also talked!

To Françoise, the word "there" was sufficient to end the entire episode. Why say more? By this time, Pierre should have been able to understand everything. He was. But that didn't stop him from wanting some further explanation.

"How did you know they were coming here today?"

"I heard them talking on the phone. When I went to call you yesterday, Aunt Elise was using the extension in your study. I recognized Perrelet's voice right away. He was going into great detail about how they would get to the spot they had chosen, the road, the point, even the woodpile. Elise kept trying to tell him all that wasn't necessary, since they would be going together. I had the feeling she was anxious to get off the phone.

Anyway, they finally agreed to meet in front of the cathedral at three-thirty. . . . "

"And you had already guessed that the Sea Gull's helper was Perrelet!"

"At first, I thought he was on his own. He admired my father and was very fond of us, you know. He was the only one I could think of who could have known Farges was using the formulas perfected by my father. I couldn't believe that he was Farges's accomplice!"

"Why didn't he say something when the estate was being settled?"

"Probably because nobody ever asked him. Just like the other workers at the plant, he went to work one day and was told that the business had changed hands. It wasn't until later that he saw all the new products he and my father had been working on."

"You mean he had copies of the formulas?"

"Maybe. Or he could have come across copies by accident. It doesn't really matter. I suppose he finally found the courage to talk to Elise and ask her what could be done."

"I can imagine how she must have shaken him up! I can hear her, now. 'Aren't you ashamed? Something has to be done!' Without her, Perrelet might never have realized he was working with a crook. He isn't very young, but he's like a child. And he's so absent-minded that Farges would never have worried about him."

"In any case, it certainly must have been Aunt Elise's idea to write anonymous letters!"

"Yes, I'm sure she wrote them, all right. She created the plans and Perrelet carried them out. The typewriter must have been his. Can't you just see Aunt Elise going over to his place every Sunday . . . and, incidentally, rearranging all his things while she was at it! That's probably how their romance got started."

"Do you think they'll get married?" asked Françoise, after a pause.

"I'm sure they will. They act as though they were married now, the way she orders him around and he does everything she says. . . . "

Slightly irritated by his last remark, Françoise stirred a little in Pierre's arms. "Do you really think Aunt Elise needs to be married to give orders?"

Pierre was sensible enough not to attempt an answer. At this late date, he was finally discovering the true value of silence. Françoise closed her eyes to enjoy the sun on her face, to feel the wind and, most of all, to allow herself to revel in the profound and simple joy that filled her heart to bursting.

She thought about Elise and Perrelet, two elderly people she had almost, for the moment, forgotten existed; yet they had been the ones who had worked so hard to make her happy. How could she tell them? But, perhaps she didn't have to. . . . With her uncanny intuition, Aunt Elise would soon realize that she and Pierre knew everything.

All the thanks Elise would ever need would be found in their eyes, in their smiles, in the way they would hug her every night. Her reward, like that of a playwright who stands backstage watching the triumph of his play, would simply be to see them happy together.

"Look," whispered Pierre.

There, high in the sky, its silver wings glorious in the golden sunlight, soared a sea gull.

HARLEQUIN MYSTIQUES

Each novel is more than you expect!

16 exciting novels
of mystery, suspense,
drama & intrigue.

See over for more exciting details.

HARLEQUIN MYSTIQUES

Romance! Suspense! Intrigue! Drama!

Awaits you in these 16 Provocative Novels . . .

. . . Harlequin Mystiques, a genuinely thrilling and engrossing concept, establishes a new high level in romantic suspense. Each novel is more than you expect — even better than you could imagine. A whole new gallery of surprising characters in chilling and dramatic situations. A riveting entertainment experience.

For an exciting, tantalizingly different reading experience, try these great new Mystiques. You'll recognize the Harlequin brand of excellence throughout each story.

See over for ordering information

Complete and mail this coupon today!

Order Form

Harlequin Reader Service
MPO Box 707
Niagara Falls, N.Y. 14302

In Canada:
649 Ontario St.
Stratford, Ont. N5A 6W2

Please send me the following Harlequin Mystiques. I am enclosing my check or money order for $1.50 for each novel ordered, plus 25¢ to cover postage and handling.

- ☐ 1. **House of Secrets**
- ☐ 2. **Vanishing Bride**
- ☐ 3. **Proper Age for Love**
- ☐ 4. **Island of Deceit**
- ☐ 5. **High Wind in Brittany**
- ☐ 6. **Love's Rebel**
- ☐ 7. **The Master of Palomar**
- ☐ 8. **Terror at Golden Sands**
- ☐ 9. **The Law of Love**
- ☐ 10. **In Search of Sybil**
- ☐ 11. **Winter at Blackfont**
- ☐ 12. **Bitter Honey**
- ☐ 13. **Sisters at War**
- ☐ 14. **The Whims of Fate**
- ☐ 15. **By Love Forgotten**
- ☐ 16. **The Sea Gull**

Number of novels checked _____ @ $1.50 each = $ _____

N.Y. and N.J. residents add appropriate sales tax $ _____

Postage and handling $ _____25¢_____

TOTAL $ _____

NAME _____
(Please print)

ADDRESS _____

CITY _____

STATE/PROV. _____ ZIP/POSTAL CODE _____

Offer expires December 31, 1978   HMY016